Laurel Lindström has had a long and rewarding career as a technical writer and journalist. She has a degree in Linguistics & English from UCLA and lives in East Sussex.

With special thanks to the lovely Kay Robinson.

The Draftsman

The Draftsman

Laurel Lindström

unbound

This edition first published in 2021

Unbound

TC Group, Level 1, Devonshire House, One Mayfair Place
London W1J 8AJ

www.unbound.com

ISBN (eBook): 978-1-78965-112-6

ISBN (Paperback): 978-1-78965-111-9

Cover design by Mecob

Printed and bound in Great Britain by Clays Ltd, Elcograf S.p.A.

To Paul, Hannah, Morgan and Matilda.
Thank you for so much happiness and so
much love.

Super Patrons

Gill Beard
Colin Bowden
Hannah Brunner
Joy Brunner
James Cairns
Judy Carayiannis
Don Carli
Christine Chambers
Mark Chapman
John Charnock
Ruth Clark
Gillian Coulson
David Dilling
William Eve
Stathis Gourgouris
Emma Green
Geoffrey Gudgion
Stephen Hardy
Mike Horsten
Mike James
Matilda Lindström

Paul Lindström
Jason Lisi
Duncan MacOwan
Claes Magnusson
Rob Mulligan
Debra Orf
Edward Orf
John Parsons
Gillian Patersom
Fiona Rasburn
Jo Reilly
Kay Robinson
Marla & Leonard Rosenthol
Diane Seaman
Helene Smith
Maya Staels
Sue Stokell
Sandra Stone
John Sweeney
Matt Thomas
Helen Tolino
Andrew Tribute
Mark Vent
Andrew Weaver
Keith and Lesley Willoughby
Candy Youngson
David Zwang

Arrivals

Through dark glasses he saw himself reflected in the rear-view mirror. And beyond his view unseen shades and colours. Tall cedar trees black against the early spring sky, reflected in glossy new red paintwork. Rain droplets distorted, outlining alien reflections, backed with red. From another life, he was sitting in a black cab and through another mirror watching his dad smoking.

Dad was telling him all about Trotsky's betrayals, miasma tales floating in the nicotine haze. A slight shake of the head, and he pushed his stick-straight hair out of his eyes, glanced back at nothing and switched off the growling engine. He threw the keys on the seat beside him. Sitting suspended in a moment, he stared at the ugly bungalow in front of him. Flat, sprawling, a spreading mass of rain-washed redbrick. Weeds and tarmac, shadows of dirty newsprint grey, offensive.

At the front door his sister was waiting in welly boots and too much scarf rising up around her neck in a wave of woolly beige. She was standing still but somehow moving, an energetic excitement shimmying and almost visible. He thinks fleeting and ugly anti-Alison thoughts, but calls out instead. 'Hey, Alison, how's it going?' Alison is large, with the same stick-straight hair as her brother. It was expertly dyed a butter mousse, burnt caramel at the roots, long and full of swing. The merging scarf gave her a curiously top-heavy aspect. She was an inverted, slightly wavering pyramid anchored in wellington boots. Tending middling to heavy she was wearing slightly too-tight trousers and a cropped cardigan under her open waxed jacket and scarf. She was cradling the phone awkwardly under her left ear while holding it with her right hand. Struggling to keep her large leather bag on her shoulder, she listed slightly as she walked towards him, ungainly and slightly knock-kneed in her rubber boots. Martin figured that whatever she was talking about probably needed a tight grip. Her husband maybe, or Joshua, more likely Martin himself.

All smiles she finished her call and beamed a gushing welcome, arms open, with heavy bag and scarf slipping in a confused tangle from her shoulder. Awkward and stomping a few paces towards him before the effort got too much, she called, 'You're here, you're finally here. It's just so exciting, isn't it, you know you're going to love it down here, don't you, you know it'll do you so much good.' Tiny whinnying titters filled the breathy spaces between her words. But the force of her enthusiasm was exhausting, and Martin was unconvinced, certain that neither of them really knew what would do him good or what would not. He looked at the graceless house he had bought six months ago and reminded himself that it was just an investment. But perhaps it could be something more, something else. He wanted to change, he had to change, had to move on, but he wasn't sure why or to what. This place of transition, of quiet, was somewhere he could perhaps ease the elastic twisted around his fervid brain, make other choices, breathe. The house, low and grovelling, looked similarly spent and empty. Unwritten space, long since exhausted, in close frigid touch with the ground. It was nearly dead. He felt his own chilled life like condensation dribbling slow and cold, moving away from him.

The bungalow was built in the sixties, a perfect square with six bedrooms, bathrooms, sitting room, dining room and kitchen, arranged along each of its four sides, with a courtyard in the centre. The rooms shared a common internal hallway, with metal-framed windows all around to let light into the house's interior. In the middle of each of the four sides a door opened out onto the courtyard. Viewed from the outside the house appeared to sprawl, the effect of its lowness to the ground and dimensions. From the inside it felt constricted, as if it were four rectangles clumsily bolted together, a prison instead of a single unified space. Surrounding it were 60 acres of parkland, woods and narrow, deep rivers that fed a pair of artificial lakes.

Turning his back while his sister fiddled with her noisy phone, Martin lit another cigarette and stared slightly dazed out across the parkland. Listless grass sloped down towards a half-mile of drive and the twisting lane running wonkily perpendicular back to the village he'd just driven through.

Pretty but with a desolate air, Catsdown had brick pavements and terraced cottages standing defiant along a busy main road, along with pollarded lime trees, four pubs, a butcher and a bakery cum tea shop. A village shop, a post office, a greengrocer's, the usual village street furniture, a letter box, signs in peeling paints over doorways, litter bins. There was a narrow set of brick steps facing the road as an aid to horse riders who couldn't reach their feet up high enough to mount on their own. Goods were displayed on stalls on the pavements, browning under a constant low-level waft of diesel particles and petrol fumes, blessings from the traffic as it continued on to more important places. As Martin nosed the Ferrari, snarling and chafing in second gear along the high street, it seemed to him that the people moved too slowly, remote and distant, soundless players on stage, trapped in a very little world.

Martin's world was expanding and he wasn't sure he liked it. It had been a huge journey to get to Catsdown, starting with that early morning trip to the Kensington car dealer and the awkward conversation with the owner. And now to be here, hours later, staring at strangers. The stranger who marked the start was a suave and elegant man, greying at the temples and with a large brown mole under one of his slightly hooded eyes. Vincent Curtis of Prestige Motors Kensington had approached Martin almost as soon as Martin climbed out of the cab.

'Could I have a quiet word, sir,' he oozed, before steering Martin towards a posh office.

Seated behind his desk, with Martin sunk deep in a leather armchair, Vincent Curtis had leaned forward with his hands clasped. There were several rings on his fingers and as he spoke, he slightly lifted and lowered his hands. Martin watched the white flash of diamonds flick back into black. Martin was being asked to allow Mr Curtis's son to manage the handover of Martin's new car. Martin couldn't see the point of the question.

'What?' he said. 'It's fine, it doesn't matter. I just want my car.'

Mr Curtis smiled expansively as he stood up, a hand extended and ignored. 'Thank you so much for your understanding. It's a family business, you see, and my son... I mean, I am keen for my son to join us. I do appreciate your understanding.'

Martin looked up at Mr Curtis, his smooth suit and impossibly white shirt and allowed himself to be ushered out of the office and into the office of the son.

Unctuous and oily with a bumped and pitted complexion, Chris Curtis at Prestige Motors of Kensington was unaware of his father's intervention on his behalf. He had no idea that clients of Prestige Motors expected something a little less callow and spotty in their motorcar salesmen. He didn't much care but he wanted to do his best, dreams of becoming a geologist notwithstanding. If he had been aware, it might have made for much less anxiety in the coming conversation. He did not see Martin exit his father's office, or perhaps he had subconsciously ignored him, preferring instead to ponder alluvial fans and floodplains.

Chris Curtis had not expected someone so close to his own age to collect the car. Martin unnerved him. He had never met the buyer of the red Ferrari F430 Coupé nor had he ever sold one over the phone before, though his father had said it was not unusual. But the money had been transferred months ago and the order went through, so here he was about to hand over the keys and paperwork to this oddly disengaged and uncommunicative young man. Chris Curtis bit at the hangnails on his thumb, anxiously struggling to reconcile the sale with the purchaser sitting on the other side of his desk. Martin looked an unlikely candidate for 4.3 litres of raw power, capable of getting from 0 to 62 in 3.9 seconds.

Slowly shuffling papers that had nothing to do with Martin, Chris Curtis had finished with his thumb. It was starting to bleed a little. Then he fiddled with his Perspex name badge, making sure it was absolutely horizontal, before rummaging in a drawer for a pen. He glanced pointlessly at the telephone, but the telephone was silent. The two of them sat, Martin motionless and Chris Curtis a mess of nervous fidgeting and sweat. He could see his father stalking the showroom floor pretending not to stare into his son's office as he adjusted the little signs on various car rooftops. As inane reworkings of soporific pop slithered along the office walls, before breathing their last and fading gently and unopposed into the carpet, Chris Curtis hummed quietly along. Martin stared and waited and started to light another cigarette.

Chris Curtis took another deep breath and let it out long and slow and with a pointed little cough asked Martin for some ID. 'You know, we have to ask, it's really more of a formality. And would you mind not smoking in here, please.' His face reddening and pulse racing, Chris Curtis tried unsuccessfully to look his client in the eye and not to be unnerved by Martin's unbroken silence as he put away his cigarettes. Picking at some spot on the back of his neck, head at an angle, an elbow held high for protection, Chris Curtis read over the passport and driving licence, quizzically tut tut tutting to himself, lips pursed tight. The tut tutting helped and his breath was easing. Gradually, his nerves were coming under control. He told himself that it had just been unexpected when Martin rolled in and said he had come to collect the car. It was just a shock, nothing more. Heads in the showroom had turned to take in this tall, slender man in his calf-length navy-blue velvet coat. They had noticed its heavy, full-skirted swing and the black boots as they slapped loud on the stylish grey and gleaming showroom floor. No one thought he was there to collect a car, not from here, not from Prestige Motors of Kensington, providers of performance cars to the discerning and extremely wealthy. But he was.

Chris Curtis's anxiety prevented him from launching into his carefully prepared patter about the car, what they had done to get it ready, the full fuel tank, the requested A to Z and the map of southeast England. His brain could only cope with thoughts of how long before the beautiful beast would be nothing more than mangled metal, a prancing horse no more. How long before it would be trapped under a bus or glittered with plate-glass exploded out of some posh shop window, passers-by standing gawping in horror at the gruesome end of a 196 mph engineering wonder. Breathe. Breathe. His customer just stared at him, watching. He didn't notice the black-heads on Chris Curtis's forehead unconcealed with pale pink concealer, or the tiny beads of sweat slowly rising to join them. Chris Curtis squeezed out an insincere and thin-lipped smile as he stood up, jiggling the single key encouragingly, trying in vain to tease. Through the office windows his father watched, bowing his head and sighing. Bobbing up and down a little more extremely than he realised, Chris Curtis ushered Martin out of the showroom towards his new Ferrari. Mr Curtis senior watched carefully as his son and Martin approached the car.

The fresh air helped and reminded Chris Curtis that according to Martin's passport he was not a boy. Twenty-six is old enough. Surely. As he opened the car door and showed his customer where the ashtray was, the waft of new car smell, all vinyl, leather and solvents, mingled with the morning air and Martin's cigarette smoke. As Martin eased himself into the deep white-leather seat, cigarette ash drifted gently down to lie in fragile and dainty comfort on a pristine red mat. He listened to what he was told, looked about the car, noted the extra keys and elaborate bunch of flowers and snapped his seat belt on. He remembered to fiddle with the mirror like his dad always did. Then he just waited for Chris Curtis to stop. Martin looked up at Chris Curtis as he closed the door and stepped away from the car, his hands clasped in silent prayer at his chest, his teeth bared in an awful grin. With a short nod, Martin clicked the key until the engine jumped alive, allowed it a momentary roar then put it in gear to inch away towards the edge of the forecourt, which seemed a very long way off. Numbers were rushing to his aid, the distance, speed, wheel rotations, fuel consumption. Numbers got him to the edge, where Martin paused, put his indicator on and listened to its satisfying binary click for a few seconds, before pulling cautiously out into the traffic. Four metres. Three miles per hour. Six. Too soon to know.

His father joined Chris Curtis as he watched Martin drive away.

'Well done, son,' he said. 'Beats geology any day, eh?'

Chris Curtis looked at his father and knew that for geology and him there was no future. No A levels and only a handful of GCSEs meant that Prestige Motors was his best hope, probably his only hope. He sighed and remembered his commission on the £165,000 sale, telling himself there were always holidays to Lyme Regis to look forward to. And the thought that if 1996 SH did by some sad chance end up under a bus or as a new feature in a shop window there might be another commission to come was even more comforting. Even more sedimentary and metamorphic holidays. Thus encouraged he waved, and as the car moved gingerly out into the seething traffic wondered what the SH stood for. And why 1996 when it was 2006.

Martin, aware of his audience, glanced in his rear-view mirror, uneasy but in control and steady on the pedals as he teased the car ahead, pressing and slipping the clutch, gradually learning how to hold it. London traffic, in its usual confused tangle, was a writhing mass surrounding him. Insidious and threatening, Martin could feel it longing to reach out and touch the car's gleaming perfection, to claim it with some ugly pinch, a bruise or graze, a kiss. But he was unexpectedly wary. Touch. The tiniest touch threatened with every movement as Martin inched along the Cromwell Road, heading west for the M4. His head was pounding and bizarre tingling cramps touched his hands and feet. A confusion of fear and ancient fragments in his brain mingled with memories of touch, of water turning cold and grey, of running lines rolling and dripping from his body as she lifted him out of the bath and into a rough and thinning towel. Touch. Loud honking from behind, and 1996 SH jumped forward, leading the herd through the now green light across a suddenly shrinking expanse of open tarmac before reaching the next halt. It took over an hour for Martin to get beyond second gear and all the while the rush in his head was screaming, screaming. And he screamed back. No. No. You can't touch me; you can't touch me now. And soon the traffic was easing and then quickly faded into the distance.

***

After the M4 and M25 his journey was peripatetic, meandering but gradually less scary. There were many halts to smoke and reconsider the route, but Martin never stopped long enough for the fear to rise. From the radio 'Crazy' was blaring 'I remember when I lost my mind', when he finally arrived at Shadowhurst many hours later. The fear was gone and in its place a sense of a monster squashed, of Martin being in control again. 'You really think you're in control?' the radio said. He switched off the engine, remembering how the ribbons of roads had unrolled ahead of him in constant invitation, tempting, daring him to keep on moving ahead, to reach out just that little bit faster, but he resisted and never was he entangled. The flashes of drivers' faces as he passed were a living cartoon, telling momentary stories, fleeting windows into other lives. The edges of the carriageway blurred the details of grit and broken glass into faceless grey as he passed. Littered debris fluttered and danced a frantic show, before falling limp and tired to wait for the next thrilling uplift and another performance. The car grumbled their soundtrack, a chorus of pistons and combustion all in time and singing curious harmonies to a shared refrain. It was the first time Martin had driven a car since he passed his test in 1997, but that was part of the purpose, the challenge. And screaming down and variously back up the A23, A22 and A21 had been just enough for Martin to win. By the time he reached Catsdown, he had already forgotten the thrill and again was the extraordinary made routine. Black and white once again prevailed.

Facing his new landscape Martin saw that the park had been left long alone. Random bramble patches, chainsawed tree stumps fractured and wounded, their broken branches drowning deep in weeds, dragged down in the rain, slowly dying and too tired to fight back anymore. But he did not see this exhaustion. He scraped out the dead cigarette with his boot, lit another and shifted slightly sideways to face the lake, lifeless and bleak. Beyond it, bordering the lane, Martin noted a sagging fence overstrewn with dead grass marking his boundary.

The original Shadowhurst Hall had been much grander, a Victorian pile that was an altogether more complicated place: three storeys high, cellars and elaborate terracing, stone stairways, balustrades, wine cellars and an orangery. Various exotic outbuildings and follies once peppered the grounds but now most of the outside structures are gone or derelict, along with the 1,000-acre farm, its barns, stables and pony paddocks all long since sold on. Old photos showed faux half-timbering and rectangular towers and a too-small front door, giving the house a pinched and mean expression. Pictures of burly men sweating in the summer heat showed them standing rigid and still in front of the house, staring black-eyed and anonymous.

When Joshua had shown him pictures of the place, Martin remembered trying to pay attention as Joshua chatted about the property. Martin and Joshua had met when Joshua's firm was instructed to advise Martin and his boss as to the options so suddenly available to them. At their first meeting Joshua and Martin's connection was instantaneous: very clever people relieved to have found not a kindred spirit, but just someone else equally bright, equally impatient. Joshua wrote the original contract and associated paperwork, dealt with the various respondents and had looked after Martin's interests ever since. Those early contracts were the start, and Shadowhurst would become the latest twist in their shared journey.

***

Joshua Fothergill is a couple of years older than Martin, but in manner he's much older. From his early twenties, Joshua had had the demeanour of a fifty-five-year-old man. He was serious, cautious, meticulous and friendless. Fresh from Oxford, he had gone straight to INSEAD to do his MBA. Paris was a curious choice for a man so old and unfrivolous in his ways, so earnest and unadventurous. But Paris would be a change at least. And there was the wine of course. Joshua loves French wines. At INSEAD his oldness and penchant for traditional English tweeds charmed his colleagues, who thought him the classic clichéd rosbif. As the course progressed they were forced to take this anachronistic freak more seriously. Joshua aced all of it, every course, from accounting and statistics through to the complex aspects of management analysis and business law. Even his electives were serious. And when he had finished his Investments and Asset Management homework, he spent evenings improving his French with a bit of Baudelaire and learning as much as he could about expensive French wines. But none of it was enough to satisfy his brain, his curiosity and competitiveness. He even tried running, which helped a bit, except that he couldn't resist sprinting past other runners. Eventually, he had discovered squash, playing three times a week at Le Club du Jeu de Paume. Fast, hard and tactical, squash was enough to exhaust him and bring everything else into focus. Squash meant that Joshua could be calm and even feign interest in trivia and small talk. Sometimes he could even flirt, although he never followed through and returned from Paris as unsullied as he had left London.

Joshua returned home with a top-flight MBA, fluent in spoken and written French and a fondness for Saint-Emilion Grand Cru. His first job landed in his lap within moments of his first interview. He was the firm's obvious choice to draft a basic contract between a lowly draftsman and one of his employer's clients. Joshua's involvement with Martin's fortunes and life had followed a steep trajectory. When he suggested Martin buy Shadowhurst Hall he had his mind on Martin's strategic investments and long-term returns on his income. It was part of his job as Martin's business manager and advisor, but when he saw the house for the first time, money was not uppermost in his mind. It was a sound investment for selling on in the future as well as a place of quiet for Martin. Joshua had come to understand the workings of Martin's peculiar intelligence, so different from the steel trap that Joshua has for a mind. But he understands not much else about Martin, despite their intimate working relationship. Martin never talks about his past. Only occasionally he communicates his curious sexual encounters, mostly to get a mess tidied up. Where Alison sees obsessiveness, Joshua Fothergill recognises Martin's compulsive need for resolutions. Black and white. True and false. He understands that there can never be greys or abstractions washing about in Martin's head. Martin is never ever distracted. Martin never ever reminisces; he doesn't look over his shoulder. Except...

If Alison saw decadence and decay, Joshua got laziness, apathy, a sense of immunity. In that he was wrong, but he did at least understand something about the static, the binary confusions, the need to see black and white resolved. Joshua's relationship with Alison was singular, part competitive, part parental, the bigger part friends united in mutual love for Martin. Joshua's impatience with Alison was no different from his impatience with most people. But he resisted his annoyance more strenuously.

Staring out again across the lakes Martin remembered when they had first talked about the house. He remembered how, careful and precise in brogues and large-check country tweeds,

Joshua had dressed to match the conversation. He had paper-clipped the house pictures to his recommendations for Martin's offer, with the newest on top and the oldest last. His soft pink lips had moved slowly behind the neatly trimmed beard and moustache, and his brow was fixed in concentration. Eyebrows tightly drawn, he had explained in careful tones what he knew of the property's history and the various investment benefits – mostly the fact that Shadowhurst is in the southeast in an Area of Outstanding Natural Beauty, so the resale value would be substantial. The conversations had bored Martin, who had no idea about buying a big house and parkland, lakes, woodland. What did he know or care. But in the end it had all led to Martin buying Shadowhurst. Joshua was in favour for the obvious reason that it was a sound investment with a likelihood of a high return. But he was also in favour because of the prospect of long weekends away from London and not at his parents' or colleagues' houses. He liked the idea of swimming in the lakes, walks to the pub and other vaguely rural pursuits he and Martin might share. Or not. Out of London there would be less noise, more intimacy and more time for those special moments Joshua always hoped were on their way. He was perpetually walking towards them. But like walking towards a massive monument from the wrong end of an endless avenue, however fast he walked he never seemed to arrive.

Martin hadn't been much interested when Joshua tried to tell him about the original house's history, how it had been requisitioned in the war, why it ended up derelict, what happened to all its parts and pieces as they crumbled and fell. But, as the original conversation came back to him in similar parts and pieces, Martin remembered that his initial resistance to the place crumbled and fell because he couldn't really think of any good reason not to buy Shadowhurst Hall. Joshua was right: this was a new opportunity and a challenge, as well as a good investment. Martin wanted something he could not specify, so he ignored the want, pushed it back and away. Was it somewhere between the money and him? Between what was and what might be? The binary choice intrigued him. And he recognised that this house might be a bridge of sorts, a bridge to somewhere elsewhere, a different space for his head to inhabit. This too intrigued him.

Martin looked back at the lake lying smooth in the still, dead air, its uncertain shades and shadows rimmed with weedy debris. He didn't see the seasonless, lifeless memories of long-gone summers shivering on its surface. Nor did he see that close to the tired fence, the twisted grasping fingers of bare trees were writing long-forgotten secrets in old blacks and sepias against a miserable sky. Martin's cigarette burned down in a series of tiny pops and hisses, masking the whispers hanging momentarily in the desolate grey air. As he stared out at the baffle of the landscape he felt a curious sense of erosion, a creeping, unidentifiable darkness. He looked again at the shades and shadows but saw only the lines between black and white.

'Are you coming in?' Alison called.

Walking towards her, Martin tossed his cigarette end into a puddle, seeing rippled reflections of the sky as its picture shifted. His footsteps were measured and slow, because he knew how much it annoyed her. She couldn't tap her foot or pace effectively in wellies, he mused.

Together and in silence they wandered slowly around the building, side by side but not too close. Alison wanting as always to reach out, Martin keeping still behind his prickly shield, denying all comers. Beyond touch. They passed forgotten flower beds full of tangled old nettles and dead grass and crossed a broken stone-twisted terrace. Carefully over uncertain cracks and lifting stones, they moved in tentative steps to the back of the house. Now the lake and a second lake, its companion, were fully visible. A grassy track linked the lakes together, bridging the dreary lawns to the fields beyond. The waters, a mirrored pair, stared at the sky, still, anonymous and blind.

The back door was unlocked and as they entered the kitchen, a wash of pale spring light flooded under the dust motes already dancing in the rays coming in from the picture windows. Keeping on her tight tweed jacket and overflowing scarf, Alison stepped neatly out of the wellies into a pair of flat pointy-toed pumps fished from the depths of her bag. She bustled across the room to lean against a shiny new Aga, gleaming, snug and cosy. It lent the space a vague warmth, but the heat could not penetrate the slate floor. Intense cold seeped up through their shoes and chilled and pinched their toes.

'Cold enough?' Alison said as Martin took in the room. It was much as he expected with the same sturdy pine table and couple of chairs that had been there when he first saw the house. But in addition he noted the large, very new fridge. It was centred in the middle of its own wall, like a shrine. Sightless and monolithic, the brushed stainless-steel deity softly hummed a cold and bloodless harmony to the Aga's gentle whispering warmth. Martin smiled as he reached out to touch the tiny black-and-white lines of brushed steel.

***

The room's quiet and chill and its soft murmurs held Martin momentarily still. He wondered if he had ever been this close to silence. He felt a curious sense of clarity and the fleeting embrace of a sensation long since lost to memory. He didn't notice a hapless sparrow hit the picture window or see the muddle of feathery brown wheel off dizzy to the safety of the nearest branch. The bird jolted Alison out of her warming moment with the Aga and she restarted the effort to give Martin her report on the house. Fixed and full of purpose she wanted to be sure he had all the facts, that he understood that she had followed his requirements for the Wi-Fi, the stereo system, the fridge, the clothes in the wardrobes, all of it.

'I've tried to follow the instructions, so I hope you've got everything you need,' she said, watching him suck on his cigarette deep and long for the last millimetres. As he stubbed it out on the draining board and pulled his fingers through the long hair flopping down over his forehead, he turned a blank look on her.

Alison held his gaze, eyes fixed, head on one side, a small smile of affection for this familiar look. To her it signified an apathetic, slightly bored trust rather than distance and alienation. She was six years older than her brother and liked to think she understood him. They stood in suspended harmony one to the other, her with her faux painted patient smile and him seeing his sister as always from a distance. Alison waited for him to reconnect. Hovering in his black jeans and tee shirt, black booted and draped as usual in dark blue velvet, he was holding onto something in his head. Patience was Alison's only option. She had no route into his headspace. But patience doesn't come easily to a woman resolutely on track almost since the moment she was born. Their parents' darling child, obsessively obedient, following the lines, looking always ahead at the next ambition, always on a mission and never once looking over her shoulder at what was behind. First it was to get the As at A level, then the university place and a double first in Art History, a degree she knew would take her into perfect husband territory. Martin's narrow and fixed path took him to an altogether other place.

Bored with the wait and taking cakes and instant coffee out of her basket, Alison looked around, slightly confused, disorientated in the new space. They heard a forced cough and the door connecting the kitchen to the rest of the house opened.

'So you're here, then. I came in at the front.'

'Ah, Simon,' she said. 'Excellent.'

Excellent? Martin wondered, unconvinced. Watching the mutual helloing, he remembered about Simon. Martin shoved his hands deep into his coat pockets and stared at the floor, waiting. A Motorola RAZR phone, his cigarettes and Zippo lighter, all reassuringly in place. The noise of the conversation battering the air was meaningless. He retreated into mental scans of his filthy penthouse up in town, curling into the memory of its safe and fetid embrace. He was here in this new and foreign space so that he couldn't be there. He was here for his stress, for his health, to change his life, to heal, to whatever, to remember, to forget, who knows. They said this house was a good idea, a sound investment, all that, all that. All that noise, all those voices and the humming buzz distant but growing louder. Fingering another cigarette, he looked up at the stranger, now silent, waiting.

Simon, shabby in worn-out work clothes and with a vaguely insolent air, looked slightly beyond Martin as they were introduced, trying to fix his gaze on the huge fridge, but his fascination got the better of him. They two were unwilling players with looks in the eye at once slightly hostile and yet resigned.

'Martin, Simon, Simon, Martin.' Alison's flailing hands gestured her introductions rather as if she were paddling a canoe.

Martin put the cigarette between his teeth and hissed 'hi', lit it and turned away to look out of the window. Simon turned in tandem and looked out of the window too, unaware that he was being ignored.

Sixtyish and newly nicked and shaved, Simon had thinning grey hair pushed and carefully sculpted back in memory of some long-gone quiff. Noticing the dead cigarette ends on the draining board and floor and the lighting of another, he cleared his throat as if to make a point. 'I'm the gardener. I do the odd jobs,' he said, mildly awkward as he looked down at the floor and the woolly outline of his grubby sock, softly beige against the floor's dense black.

Martin still stared away and said, 'What gardening?'

Simon had no ear for irony. 'I just do, always have, it's what I do for the place. Mowing mainly. Hedges. Wood. That sort of thing.'

Martin turned his head to look at him. 'Wood. Okay,' he said, slow nodding in total incomprehension and remembering that keeping Simon on was not a choice. It was part of the sale: Simon came with the house and could keep his job until he was ready to retire. 'Are you planning to retire soon?' Martin asked and Simon pulled his hand through his hair, feigning sheepishness but grinning back an adamant 'no, sir' with impertinence barely concealed. The job interview was over. Still smiling, Simon said, 'I'll be here for as long as you want me. Well, at least until teatime.'

Martin turned to his sister. 'Is there milk in the fridge so that we can have a cup of tea?'

Alison forgot the daffodils she was arranging. 'Cup of tea? What? But you don't drink tea. Since when do you want tea?' Her staccato questions rose in pitch as they ran along, interspersed with tight, breathy laughs, her own uncertain punctuation. Eventually, the questions were lost in the tinselly squeak she usually reserved for cocktail parties with her husband's business colleagues and clients.

Martin, already at the fridge, had the answer to his own question. Ignoring his sister, Martin looked at the coffee and cakes on the counter and said, 'Nor is there tea.' He saw that the fridge did have the twenty-four bottles of Pol Roger champagne he'd requested, along with stacks of small tins of tuna fish in brine. Good. Turning to Simon he stared a moment at him and his now upstanding grey hair and handed over an untidy bundle of notes. 'Go and get some for us, would you. Take the car. Key's on the seat. Oh, and get me a bin as well. Get bins for all the rooms. All the same, small and chrome. Get them delivered if you can't fit them in the car.'

'Are you sure, sir?' Simon replied, hesitant and glancing out of the window at gleaming red, hard-shelled perfection. It looked almost alive, pawing the ground, and was surely rabid with lethal manic tendencies. 'I'm more a Mondeo man myself,' he mumbled, staring at the car. He glanced down again at the holey socks and, spreading his grimy hands, remembered the muddy boots waiting for him by the front door. Not keen he thought, not keen, but Martin was still gazing at him, just waiting.

'It's Martin,' Martin said, 'just Martin. We'll need about a dozen, one for here and one each everywhere else.'

Alison was confused. 'Bins? Are you serious? Bins were not on the list' was the best she could come up with. Martin ignored her and watched Simon slope off to get his boots and prepare to do battle with the Ferrari and the bins.

Alison, with her daffodils nodding in their jar, let her fingers twitch and pluck at them. She was talking half to herself in a series of low-level little clucks and chortles, wondering if this thing with the tea and the bins meant change of a sort. It was almost certainly out of character, almost ordinary, she muttered. She kept pinching and pulling at the flowers, her head on one side then the other, furtively watching Martin, looking for tangible hints of change. She saw none.

Martin, unaware of her sly glances, was fixed instead on the alien, faceless space around him and the whispers he thought he heard. He looked at his mobile phone. Whispers not fizz, echoes not static. Curious. There was no signal, no sign of missed calls or messages, and somehow this was a good thing. He lit another cigarette and looked towards the stillness beckoning from the rooms beyond.

Alison noticed him absentmindedly check the phone and asked, 'Have you got signal?'

His phone back in his pocket Martin stared through the question and said, 'Is the Wi-Fi set up?'

'Well, yes, like you said you wanted it, top of the line and that's what's been installed. State of the art. I sent you a text with the code. Try it on your Mac,' she replied uneasily.

'No. Don't know. Don't worry about it. I don't need it now.'

And Alison was once more confused as she watched him stare out again, although he did not see the gloomy afternoon as it shuffled off into the shadows beyond the kitchen windows.

She joined him and put her hand under his arm. For a fleeting moment she was snug against the stick-thin arm in its velvet sleeve before he pulled away. Side by side they watched Simon jolt along the drive for a few metres, before suddenly letting go and disappearing around the bend. Martin's lips curved almost imperceptibly into the slightest of smiles as he remembered what it felt like that morning, driving the new car from the showroom in South Kensington. He had not jolted but the creature had terrified him, a satisfying, cathartic terror, his reward. After a lifetime in the backs of black cabs, he'd set himself the task of driving to his new house alone, which required buying a car, collecting it, finding his way out of London and into the right county unaided, before tracking down his new address. All of this he had done, ordinary and yet thrilling.

In the kitchen Alison was talking again, her voice slow and low, not wanting to distract him too suddenly. He sat down at the kitchen table, patient and listening to the binary static slowly rising in his brain. He was waiting for that inevitable and reliably reassuring Alison conversation. It's the conversation she needs to have with him so that she can be sure of him, will be able to let him go for a little while, let go her anxiousness at least for a little while. At least until next time. It's the wallpaper conversation, the one about what happens next and why and how and who, and it absolutely doesn't have to be a dialogue. It's a habit they share, so Martin knows that the occasional grunt will do by way of acknowledgement, just so that she knows he is listening. That is all she needs for reassurance, for some sort of absolution, forgiveness, though she does not know why. Ever was it thus with them; locked memories and buried, unseen secrets.

Alison sat down, deliberate and slow, and picked up her pen. She started going through her list, her voice getting slightly louder as she marked off each item. She threw in the occasional hum for added impact and between hums she spoke slowly, ponderously, aware that Martin wouldn't pay attention yet. But she wanted his attention. The conversation had to begin with an opening act, the warm-up for a one-man band, in anticipation of the main event. 'Shopping. Feed store. Petrol.' Alison had to have visibly ticked off at least four items before she could expect a response, even a grunt. Get house keys from solicitor's. Tick. Order and oversee installation of oversized stainless steel fridge freezer. Tick. Make sure ice and water dispenser fully functioning. Tick. Almost fill fridge with bubbly. Tick. Add forty-eight small tins of tuna fish. Tick.

Five ticks later Martin, another cigarette on the go, nodded and said, 'Yes, it's fine' as he watched her check through the list, eyes narrowed and immaculate nails gleaming coral pink. Without looking up she dropped her voice to a half-whisper so that he had to pay attention. Eyes still narrowed and fixed downwards on her list, head to one side, she said in a distracted, slow mumble, almost a monotone as if they were trading secrets, 'You need to tell me if the furniture is as you want it, so that we can get it moved if you don't like it where it is.'

Martin almost just agreed, but momentarily assertive he stood up. A shaky hand brushing specks of ash from the dark blue velvet, he headed off out into the hall and towards the sitting room. Alison rose slowly and picked up the cigarette he had left on the edge of the table. Nurturing it over a cupped hand, she dropped it into the sink, ran the tap for a second and followed her brother.

The sitting room at Shadowhurst is not particularly large. L-shaped with an open fireplace at one end, the long side has two sets of double-glazed doors opening out onto the terrace. The views across the once unkempt lawns to the lakes and fields with woodland beyond are still broad and generous, in stark contrast to the dwarfish house. Standing there on that first day, Martin felt the house's slow, low breath, its hollow sigh, that curious calm again. Perhaps it was the quiet. In the stillness the fizzing static racing around his brain seemed to slow to something less familiar, more a sort of muffled hiss. Together they stood on the terrace looking out across an overgrown mess of gardens in various flat and dead green shades. Beyond the beds they saw lichen-pitted and measled-grey statuary, heads bent to share sad forgotten confidences. Shivering and friendless maidens were leaning in the lazy chill, brambles shoved aside heraldic lions, clawless in decline and too feeble to fight back. Marooned stonework lay powerless and silent, weeds and molehills were moving on towards different and more energetic conversations. Motionless they watched as the lakes rippled occasional teasing patterns of watery blacks and greys under a whispered breeze. The air tiptoeing across the surface left in its wake a hint of subdued sparkle, of something silent, hidden and unspoken, a whisper. But Martin did not hear it. It might have been the long-lost glimmer of an idea floating for a brief while before sinking away, away from the light. The woods beyond the lake, bare and friendless, their naked branches reaching into rising mists, seemed to be waiting. A story to tell. Martin saw none of this and turning back into the room, he said, 'It's all fine, really it is, you've done what I want.'

Alison sighed and smiled, calm and reassured. Released once more, at least for a little while.

Martin's sitting room was carpeted with the thickest possible white wool with super-insulated underlay. Its expensive expanse was disturbed only by a single very large black nubuck leather sofa, dressed up with gaudy velvet cushions scattered in reds and purples. When Martin first saw them he raised an eyebrow at Alison, an interruption she felt before she looked up involuntarily from her list.

'I know, I know you didn't ask for them, but I thought you'd like them, especially in velvet.' A moment's pause. 'I can take them away again,' she ventured.

'No. Don't. They're fine. It's all fine.'

Turning away from the colour, he saw the wall-mounted McIntosh amp, receiver, turntable, CD player and the shelf of CDs lined up like soldiers waiting for orders. All there. He smiled slightly and appreciated Alison's placement of the sofa centred at the perfect listening distance, his vinyls close by on a shelf out of the light and well away from the fireplace.

'It's fine,' he said and sat down. 'No need to change anything.' Another cigarette lit only momentarily before he threw it into the dead grate.

Alison, shocked again, managed to smile and check herself. 'Good. It's going to work out, you know, it's going to be fine.'

Martin wasn't sure what to do with his hands and looked back, his face once more a blank, placing his hands tight on his knees. She noticed his face's too early lines, the shades of faded breeze-block grey, and the usual vague broodiness darkening his expression. He went and looked out of the windows behind her. He didn't see the afternoon shadows creeping across the lake, slowly drawing into darkness. He saw no greys. Birds were hurrying home, cheeping and piping loud and shrill their goodnights. The birds' urgent cries lanced sharp across the greying dusk. He heard the screams and the silence.

'Joshua, is that you... Oh good, yes he's here. I know. It's probably on silent.' Handing the phone to her brother as he watched the slowing light, she said, 'It's Joshua. He rang before, just when you were arriving.'

Martin looked at the phone a moment, before deciding to take the call. 'Hiya... Yes, it's weird... hmm... Yeah... No, not much... Are you coming down?' Martin wasn't really sure if he wanted Joshua to come down or not, but he knew he should ask. He'd been told that he should ask, because this is polite and polite is what Joshua expects. It had never occurred to Martin that other people might expect it too.

Joshua had given him the little lecture about manners after the last incident at the London flat, the time with that one, that one with all the chaotic blonde hair. Martin had misread everything about the situation, inviting an overly familiar, agenda-driven stranger into his filthy flat. There had been an unexpected and sudden turn from flirting prospector to fire-breathing demon. Martin's flat was not as expected and his guest, horrified by the grunge and terrible stench, was knocked totally off track. 'What do you mean, you don't want sex? We can just do it here,' Martin had said, gesturing to his unmade bed with its landscape of oily alien stains and crusted creases. In his anxious guest the heart rate was rising.

Joshua arrived as the conversation hit a precipice, along the lines of 'I thought we were going somewhere.' 'No.' The big blonde backing out of the flat as Joshua was coming in unexpectedly felt Joshua's body warm and solid. This had only ramped up the fear and the volume. Joshua was standing still, bemused and patient, and closing the door behind him. He gently patted at the air before raising his hands in mock surrender. Martin declined to fill in any details or make introductions, standing instead stock still, scowling and annoyed. What was the problem? Joshua looked at the germophobic fool and saw yet another excessively lunched and liqueured individual, one who was very drunk and whose mood had apparently swung from aroused anticipation to overwhelming revulsion and confusion. Joshua had to admit the flat did look more inner-city slum than posh penthouse. And the smell was gag inducing.

Joshua sighed and waited for the tears and declarations of heartbreak that would be coming along momentarily. It was all part of the performance. He tried to calm the blubbing mess of snot and acrimony and disgust. Joshua carefully took an elbow and turning towards the hallway he gently ushered their visitor out. He handed over the readies by way of a gift and an apology and 'so you can get a cab home. Goodbye.' Martin handed Joshua his ringing phone to answer and leaned against the doorjamb, watching. The sobbing slowly subsided and his no-longer-friend wobbled off in slow and uncertain steps towards the lift, surreptitiously counting the notes. Martin listened as Joshua told Alison mostly what was going on. Alison had listened slightly confused, yet unsurprised, and then she had told Joshua about Shadowhurst.

***

Shadowhurst had belonged to one of Alison's husband's cousins, a woman whose taste in lifestyles and people tended to guileless and usually disappointing excess. It was a sorry trail of feathers flounced, plucked and faded and reality's brutal, sharp flint. Alison's husband's cousin had insisted on this massive square bungalow, its arctic rooms and the then elegant grounds, with some idea that she and her husband could play country squire and his lady and be happy again. But their feathers and flint lifestyle involved too many ill-conceived investments, unexpected costs and repairs for things you'd never think need mending like terraces and hedges. Too many more expenses for invisible necessaries, like sewage collection and heating oil. All of it was beyond the means of feathers and flint, no matter how graceful or sharp. Too little money, too many bad choices, too much denial, too few options. Same old boring litany of disintegration and slow decline.

When the husband pegged it, Alison's husband's cousin had no choice but to face her own denials, though she did not at first see them. 'It's all fine, of course it is,' she would say, hanging up on concerned relations before twisting open a bottle of ever cheaper gin. It's so much more genteel than vodka or whiskey, she would tell herself, sitting alone on the sofa, wiping at smudged mascara and reapplying lipstick with not quite enough precision. It didn't matter. No one was ever there to see her crying at the television and passing out on the bathroom floor.

At Christmas cocktails with one of her sympathetic neighbours and over the top of her sadly empty glass, Alison's husband's cousin told Alison that she wanted to sell up. The confidence came almost as soon as Alison was in range. 'The place is just too much for me without him, you know, it's just too much,' her husband's cousin had explained, sucking on a lemon slice and eyeing up the party bar. Later she reminded Alison again, this time ending her sentence with a confidential hick and a small snort as she repeated with a sage nod, ''ez jus too mushnow.' She was weaving slightly, wild-eyed and her colour rising to two perfect circles of red on her cheeks and a daub of red moustache across her upper lip. She pushed back her blonde-streaked hair, arched her eyebrows and made wide her eyes, and asked Alison to join her for a sneaky fag. She put a wavering finger almost to her lips before ambling off out of range of Alison's withering disdain, which she hadn't noticed.

Alison, empty sherry glass in hand, had been about to give Roger the nod that it was time to leave his client's party and go home. She was irritable, her mind elsewhere, wondering what to do about her brother, his grungy lifestyle, his appalling health and his perpetually fragile state of mind. And why did those incidents with strangers keep happening? What did he do to get it so spectacularly wrong? And why did she never get to meet any of these people? Did he even have them in his life or were they just a lonely series of unfulfilling one-night stands? Perhaps Shadowhurst might be an answer to at least part of the puzzle. She went out into the garden to where her husband's cousin was dragging fruitlessly on a shrunken dog-end, looked her in the eye and said, 'I might have an answer. Let's see what I can do.' A childish smile spread across her husband's cousin's face before, with an incoherent mumble, she sank gracefully into a small shrub that was not so small that it couldn't accommodate her slow and dignified slide into the flower bed's soft embrace. Empty glass in hand she continued to smile benign and content in the general direction of her cousin's wife and her cousin's wife's remarkably similar-looking companion.

What Alison could do was what brought Martin to Shadowhurst and her husband's cousin to a new and fortunately faraway life. As Alison's husband's cousin put it on a postcard, she was roaming 'somewhere altogether elsewhere, like Auden's caribou'. Alison had no idea what she was on about and didn't much care.

Turning from the light fading into the lake, Martin handed her phone back and said, his voice emotionless and flat, 'He's coming down tomorrow.'

'That's good. He'll be able to help you decide what else you need.'

'It's okay. It's all fine. I don't need anything. He just wants to see the place. Hang out.'

Alison pictured Joshua coming down tomorrow, arriving in a London taxicab all the way from Hampstead, with the meter steaming. He'd dress the part, she knew, with the brogues and possibly one of those long waxed riding coats with the little shoulder cape, dark green, a suitable countryside disguise. Would he also bring a quilted Barbour jacket and wellies, she wondered. Would he stay the night here in the house? She continued to make notes on her list, and Martin wandered off to inspect the room that had convinced him about the house in the first place.

A glass addition to the main building, the room projects out over the steepest parts of the lawns, drawing the eye down to the lakes. It is completely made of glass: glass roof, glass walls, glass doors and resting as light, almost floating on a pale and golden expanse of beech wood floor. The glass goes top to bottom, edge to edge, side to side and over. The walls and windows are the same and give a vaguely wavering view of the space beyond. The views on each of the three sides are different, but they all really might be the same as far as Martin is concerned. When it rains Martin watches the water running rills, ripples and wavy lines, rolling down across the surfaces lurching into the gutters all around. The gutters are the only breaks in the glass between the windows of ceiling and walls. They are too small, so they don't carry much water. Instead, the water bounces fitful and urgent, undisciplined and chaotic like a band of rowdy children dancing madly across the surfaces. The water runs skidding off out of bounds to the edges of a watery world, so when it rains Martin watches the world dappling grey and searches for black and white, through light and glass and water. He watches random urgent patterns twisting and then meandering elsewhere. He watches endless shifting pictures beyond white noise, curious imaginings that can never resolve into black and white. They cannot touch him, yet they are messages only Martin can read.

Blank and faceless, the glass still reflects an uninterrupted view. The scene is still open. Standing in the centre of the room that first day, Martin saw again the long, sloping lawns, his eye journeyed slowly down to a small valley and up the other side to a line of woods and muddled undergrowth. He decided he wanted sheep on the slope. They could graze across his lawns and fields, just as many as needed so that no one had to mow. They would break up the great expanse of green, differentiate it. He could get some black and some white ones. They would move about in random patterns he could count and predict. The lake was almost motionless now, silent, a secret hidden in the fading light. An air of slight foreboding was rising as the late afternoon darkened and turned to evening, something teasing and staring a brooding challenge as the waters stirred slightly and a whispered breeze softly sighed. But Martin didn't hear it.

Simon and Sheila

Sitting at the wheel of the Ferrari, Simon took a deep breath and wondered where to put the key. Staring at it and then at the dashboard, he put the key back down beside him on the passenger seat and took tight hold of the steering wheel. Clasping it and raising his fingers one by one to study his filthy nails again, his grip started to ease. Slowly he felt his hands soften to caress a thing of beauty, somehow urgent and provocative, he knew it was yearning for him. All he had to do was to put the key in the ignition. He picked it up, reached out tentative and slow, hesitating and struggling a moment – come on, come on – his fingers shaking before thrusting the key into its slot. Firm and determined he turned it and with a couple of clicks felt the pulse of another being surge through his body, the sound and touch of it rose and swarmed, a caress so terrifyingly dangerous that, breathing fast, he had to switch the engine off again. As he watched open-mouthed, his hovering fingers suspended and still reaching out to the key, he wondered if he could pull this off. Can he actually start this Ferrari for real, steer it and drive it to the village to buy milk and tea and a dozen chrome bins? Will the shop have that many? Will they fit in the back of the car? Enough distractions, and suddenly reckless and Teddy-boy bold he turned the key once more.

A surge of long-lost aggression and his foot stamped the pedal right down to the floor, answering the engine's snarling roar with his own primal deep-throated scream, rising unbidden. Head shaking, his mouth wide, tongue on chin, the face a contortion burying his tearing eyes. The revs surged into the red before his foot eased off and the engine, reluctant and compliant, grumbled down to a steady pulsing rhythm. Shocked, his breath deep and heavy, Simon's mouth collapsed into an idiotic smile, widened and turned into an ugly leer. His hands stroked the steering wheel up and down, up and down. Relieved and afraid his moment would pass, Simon squared his shoulders, heard the engine's rumbling tease, sly and imploring for more, and put the car in gear with barely a touch on the gearstick's smooth silver head.

Sweating and slightly dizzy, exhilarated as the Ferrari roared, eager and impatient to move, Simon was breathing in rapid shallow breaths. The accelerator pedal, barely grazed with the toe of his muddy boot, brought him an unexpected head rush and slight dizziness. The car lurched forward in a series of small leaps before Simon's chafing toe could balance the slide consistently between the accelerator and the clutch. He let intoxication reach up from his feet through his legs and hips and back and down his arms into his clutching hands, completing the tingling adrenaline circle that was taking them forwards. He steered into a too-tight curve before straightening and surging off down the drive. Somewhere in his head he was still Simon, but everywhere else in his body he was in love, his senses and emotions barely under control. Leaning into the acceleration pushing into the small of his back, he glanced warily in the mirror at the disappearing view and shifted from first to second gear, with a fingertip and a flick of the wrist.

Simon was not used to feeling youthful or foolish. But he didn't care now about the muddy boots or the fingerprinted paintwork. His love was leading him, wanton and loose, down the lane at 50 miles an hour. Still in second gear, a glance at the speedometer and the hedges passing by far too quickly, he realised that the terror was more than he could take, despite love's charms. His guilty moment had been fleeting, an echo of someone long since gone, even though there had been no such person in his life, not even the idea of one. He'll be wanting a kettle too, he mused as he reverted to his usual meandering driving style. Simon's driving style was suited to his inclination to flatten any wayward pheasant or pigeon, or even mouse, foolish enough to amble onto the road, so he rarely kept a steady line. But this habitual entertainment could be problematic for this particular journey, so he kept straight and hoped nothing would stray into his path. The mess would probably be a lot and hard to hide, it might even make a dent.

Approaching his cottage some half a mile up the lane Simon, cavalier with an arm draped roguish and wanton across the back of the passenger seat, pulled up with a sharp little screech and hit the horn. His wife peered out from an upstairs window and hurried down, while Simon coaxed the engine into a series of excited little revs, a promise to keep his secret safe. As he waited he watched with satisfaction an approaching horse rider pull up and take an alternative route through the woods, instead of continuing on the lane. Simon's swaggering vanity chose to believe the detour was to avoid Simon and his scary car. That it was the loveliness of riding into woods and not on the road never occurred to him.

'What's this? Who's let you loose on this monster?' Sheila gawped and stared fish-eyed and slightly horrified.

'Your new boss. Get your coat,' Simon replied. 'He's wanting stuff from the village and it's getting late so get a move on.'

Folded up staple style in the deep bucket seats and strapped in tight, Sheila asked, 'So what's he like. When am I expected?' She was mildly interested to meet her new boss, but she didn't really care. The boundaries of her life had been fixed long ago, she knew what she wanted and that for most of it, she had had her way. Now she had reached an age of contentment, satisfied in her world and confident that nothing much was worth getting worked up about. For Sheila, life's uncertainties were no longer anything to be feared, no longer threatening. Martin and Shadowhurst was just work, just another bloke in the big house wanting her to keep it clean, the latest in a short chain that had been growing link by link since the old house was pulled down and the new one put up.

***

The Mainwarings had been there first, with all those rowdy children and the mad parents, who let the kids run loose all summer long and in all the holidays, before sending them back to boarding school. Sheila remembered the time when she noticed flames coming from the garden shed as she was hanging the washing on the line. 'Mrs Mainwaring,' she'd shouted, 'the shed's on fire!'

Mr Mainwaring came rushing out from his glass studio and called to his boys, 'Oy! What's going on!', just in time to see a small explosion and three of his five sons come running onto the lawn, one of them clutching his hand and screaming. 'Dad, quick, Michael's blown his hands up.' Much commotion and shouting to someone to call an ambulance and the dogs barking and Michael still screaming as he emerged, singed and sooty from the smoke, blood pouring in sudden crimson splashes on the bright green lawn. Sheila had reached him first, wrapping his hands, fingers adrift, tight together in a newly laundered pillowcase. Blood bloomed sudden, fast and greedy across its whiteness. She held his hands and fingers more firmly, watching the flow slow as the blood seeped into big red droplets moving out into the light, to shine fresh and bright in the sunshine. And brave Michael, tipping at the edge of childhood, doing his best not to cry anymore, hiccupping and gasping, anxious and staring in horror at the pillowcase in terror of what it held and fearful of what his dad would say about the destroyed shed. Tears continued to fall, but a wicked look stayed in his eyes as he glimpsed back at the demolished mess, a rising thrill of power and excitement mingled with pain and adrenaline.

Sheila remembered the washing and how she watched the smoke breathing its grubby breath on her clean sheets as she held tight the boy's hands. The linens were already picking up specks of black and grey, shining silhouettes on the sullied white fluttering in the smoke-smudged air. She remembered the other boys, all breathless and excited, wide-eyed and shocked and impressed, piling into the car with their mum and dad to follow Michael in the ambulance. She remembered later how Mrs Mainwaring had still been in shock and, sipping incessantly at a paint-stained jam jar brimming with warm white wine, could only repeat how boys shouldn't try to make their own fireworks because that was a man's job. They just shouldn't – sip sip – they just should leave that to the men – sip sip. Sip sip all the way to bedtime. When Sheila told Simon about it over their tea, he said, 'One of them boys had it coming, just a question of which one and when', nodding and smug because neither of his children would have ever done anything so dangerously stupid or shown such reckless imagination.

When Michael came back from hospital for the last time some weeks later, he had a reconstructed thumb and forefinger on one hand and missing ring and little fingers on the other. He bounced up to Sheila and said, halfway between a squeak and a growl, 'Could you teach me to knit', before waggling his bandaged hands in her face. Sheila didn't get the joke and carried on ironing as Michael tiggered his way out into the garden. When the Mainwarings moved down to Cornwall to found an artists' collective, she had been glad to see the back of them and their raucous energy. Good riddance, she said.

Art wasn't Sheila's thing, at least not the art you couldn't recognise. Her ideas were simple, no nonsense, black's black, white's white. And there are no greys. But, unlike Martin, the black and white is not the bars of a cage. They are simply all she sees. At a vague sixtyish, Sheila, like her husband with his receding quiff and bumptious attitude, looked pretty much the same as she had when he met her all those decades gone, only slightly bigger and wrinklier and greyer. She was still anonymous, secure in her world where nothing changed much. The sixties psychedelia and colours in general had passed her by. The seventies had just been silly, although she did still like to hear some of the music when it came up on the radio of a Saturday. Her clothes were still sensible, plain and slightly dingy, even when they were new, and always too big because she liked to be comfy. Her air of resolute, disinterested oldness had always been there, even when she was young. A handsome young man suspicious of giggly girls and their mysterious expectations, Simon did not see a dowdy young woman. He did not see a girl too soon time-textured and greyed, but someone mature, exotic and irresistibly sophisticated. He saw a woman worthy of what he thought was his maturity, his handsomeness and his timeless style.

For Simon it had started long before they ever stepped out together. He had loved Sheila ever since that summer evening in the village hall when the war was newly over, when the land and the people were still shocked and broken. There had been that disappearance, a disappearance that turned out to be an elopement and everyone talked about how romantic it was. Everyone was called and Sheila's mum had been helping with the tea and cakes and then the clearing up. Sheila was nine years old and Simon was twelve. 'Has anyone any information that could help us?' the police had said. 'Does anyone know anything about this Canadian airman?' She and Simon, bored and unable to grasp even slightly what was going on, had hidden together under the trestle tables. Peering out from behind the tablecloths, they were untying men's shoelaces and trying to smear the ladies' fake seams without them noticing. In their stealthy mischief they never spoke, looking out at the sea of shoes and legs and just knowing what should happen next and doing it. After all the laces within reach were undone and the pencilled seams smudged without anyone noticing, they had wandered out into the soft summer air. They sat eating crumbly dried egg cake on the steps of the village hall, hearing the blurred sounds of anxious discussions and oblivious to everything beyond their cake, the steps beneath them, the fading sun's gentle embrace and each other.

***

They married when they were still in their teens, when he first started sporting the Elvis quiff and the buttons of his shirt were always undone just that little bit too far. Quite why this preening man had fallen for her, Sheila never really knew, still didn't, even though she remembered that night at the village hall and how suddenly it had ended when the people came flooding out and they had to move off with their parents into the chill of dusk to go home. Today he still had the same look, except that the wavy quiff was grey and sparse, the shoulders not so sharp and those opened buttons teased for a swollen, grey-wisped belly. She had never really left that moment all those years ago, their beginning. The two of them had rubbed along for many years, content, patient and arguing no more or less than the next, surviving their ups and downs because the alternative didn't bear thinking about; there was no alternative for them. Any random excitements that came their way were never so exciting as that warm summer's night in 1945. They were swiftly absorbed into the fabric of their shared and largely contented lives to disappear without a trace. Sheila and Simon had always lived within a five-mile radius of where they and their two children, long since flown, were born. Simon and Sheila were together at peace with their lot, inclined to laziness, addicted to television, the gentle rhythm of the rural year and each other's quiet and unchallenging company. They were untouchable.

Twisting in her too-deep seat, and in her baggy dress and coat, Sheila observed that 'there's not much room for shopping' and, apart from assisting with the bin buying and fitting them all in the car, that was the extent of their conversation. When he dropped her back at the cottage after the excursion, she briefly wondered why ever people wanted to spend their money on such impractical things as this silly small, red car. The thought was gone in a moment. 'Don't be late,' she said, before shutting the gate behind her and heading for the kitchen to get the tea ready in time for the news.

By the time Simon got back to Shadowhurst, a gloomy darkness was turning the house's colours into murky toneless shades. He noticed a slender curl of smoke reaching from the chimney and stretching upwards and mingling with the growing dusk, turning purples and greys slowly into black. Joshua had warned Simon that his new boss was just as likely to leave again as not, so the fire he took as a sign that Martin would stay, at least for the night. There were no other lights on as Simon called through the empty kitchen, 'Where do you want the bins?' In silence he lined them up along one wall in a tidy shining row marking the edge of the kitchen floor. The daffodils he transferred along with the water, which he took great care not to spill, from their jar into a new vase, their yellow trumpets bobbing untidily. The new kettle was slowly filled and switched on. All of these movements, deliberate and careful executions, repeats of familiar patterns, are details, markers, that Simon understands, guards and keeps near. That they are a buffer to hide behind, a means to avoid uncertain challenges, never occurs to him. Simon inhabits a prescribed and finite space, a place of safety, somewhere predictable. The routine is his shield.

Watching the kettle as it came to a boil, Simon made a mental note to warn Sheila. She must not smirk or stare at the long blue velvet coat or the knee-high black leather boots when she comes to see Martin tomorrow. He's their boss and they want to keep him steady and in the neighbourhood, instead of leaving unexpectedly for some new life in Cornwall or wherever, messing up the continuity, making waves, disrupting the lines. Simon's looked after this estate since his teens, when he helped his dad and granddad. Sheila and her mum before her have always done for Shadowhurst Hall. That's how it is, that's how it will be. The kettle's boiling.

All these thoughts were crowding Simon's head and making him feel tired, as he kicked off his boots and sloped across the kitchen, along the hall to the sitting room. There they were, sitting staring at the fire and Alison's saying, 'How long will he be staying. Where will he sleep?' As Martin turned, shaking back the hair, he ignored her and called back, 'Where are the bins? I want them in here.' To Alison he said, 'I don't know. As long as he wants. He can sleep where he likes.' The bins being brought in distracted her enough not to be annoyed by Martin's disinclination to engage or confused by his apparent assertiveness and his desire for bins.

'Brilliant. You got chrome ones. Line them up over there by the windows.'

Doing as he was told, Simon said, 'Kettle's boiled and I'm off. It's late. If that's okay?'

Martin nodded without looking at him, so Alison walked with him back into the kitchen.

'Thank you,' she said. 'My brother's a little overwhelmed by it all.'

Simon looked at her, slightly bewildered, and mumbled, 'Right, well, goodnight, Alison', and closed the kitchen door behind him.

Alison filled the pot, picked up the change Simon had left on the table and called to Martin to come and have some tea. The two of them sat silent, chewing their biscuits looking at the plate and the cups, Martin barely aware that he wasn't smoking.

'Are you off the fags, then, Martin?' Alison joked, expecting him to immediately light up. But instead he nodded and hissed yes through his sixth chocolate digestive, crumbs flying across the table and peppering their tea. With a malevolent look through the floppy fringe he changed his mind and shot back, 'No, not always, just here I think. You're right, this place is good. But I need it to be different, completely different.' Slightly perturbed, Alison could not answer, so taking a swallow of tea, she waited for him to continue. Silence. She understood that conversation was over for the day.

'I'm off, then,' she said, knocking back the dregs and standing full of purpose and focused intent. Alison gathered up her bag and scarf, putting them into her basket along with her pumps, before stepping into her wellies. No trace left of sister Alison, apart from the slight feint of her concern hanging on the air as she smiled and turned away, knowing better than to venture a hug. In her too-tight trousers and cashmere cardie and pearls, Alison had turned full-face away from her brother as soon as their conversation stopped. She was taking on a new mask and the view of her husband's wife was one that she had seen in the mirror since childhood. Poised and in control, with a power to compel, a power to progress whatever task she undertook to its required conclusion. An iron-willed little girl pouting and flouncing and telling herself that she was not like her family, that she was different, probably a foundling or a hospital mix-up and an imposter in their show. This is why she could love her peculiar baby brother, even though he never spoke to her or to their mother. She was always aware that he needed her protection because he was strange, and in the last few years, since Martin's money, their parents' death and her marriage, this unfulfilled conceit was finding its place. All the pieces in her life were in place, so Alison was ready to really be Martin's sister, to fulfil the role, to help him. 'Now is the time,' she had told herself. The foundations of her life and the fulfil-ment of that childhood self were a reality they both could share and enjoy, once Martin was better, when he was more normal, more like her. It was a hope borne of vanity.

Alison was the essence of expectations for the wives of wealthy country men, and for the mothers of their children. Her confection was one of ambition and rigid adherence to her own code, the one that told Alison that she was absolutely in control and that nothing could thwart her, not even her brother. Alison never understood that she could manage Mar-tin's peculiarities only because he allowed it, and only because they both recognised that somewhere in his life he needed her. But maybe that wasn't forever. Martin saw his sister in her own uniform, but never questioned it because she was always just there, always on time, yet always late in her understand-ing, with a roving blind spot that randomly blocked her view. Sensible, reliable, efficient and mostly able to make the right choice, understanding and accepting what she was told but only as long as it conformed to her view. Listening was no part of Alison, who heard selectively. If something fits her narrative, Alison never questions, never has doubts or any curiosity for alternative ideas. She doesn't consider the motives of others as long as those others fit within an Alison convention. 'He needs me, don't fret, love,' her mother had said and Alison believed it. Sightless beyond her view, Alison is the sort of woman who always has tissues in her bag, always has change for parking and always has a fully charged phone. She lives still according to her mother's advice to always be prepared, always plan ahead and always be in control. But Alison didn't see, couldn't see.

***

As he heard the door close, Martin sighed and leaned into the flock of garish cushions. He held up his shaking hands, mildly fascinated that they could make such a commotion. He turned to watch the fire flickers dancing in a chorus line on the chrome of the bins, a row of flame against the fading light beyond. More soldiers lined up and waiting for action. The room was dark and slowly warming; Alison had put on the central heating before she left and the chill was loosening its intense grip. He considered taking off his coat, but the intimacy with the space was still too much. Instead he went back to the kitchen, finished off the biscuits and cracked a Pol Roger.

Champagne in hand he moved slowly along the hallway that led around the central courtyard. It was filled with broken bits of flowerpots, some crumpled plastic sheeting, a leaning barbecue beseeching on bended knee. He hadn't noticed the courtyard before and hadn't told Alison what to do about the space. It appeared to carry reminders of some sad history, a jumbled departure, and this disturbed him so he turned away. He wanted no hints of other people's lives, he wanted only an empty canvas at which he could just stare. Except. Moving down past his glass room, he checked two of the six bedrooms and continued along into the main hallway and the front door. The outside lights Simon had left on beckoned into the night's lignin black. Turning them off, he faced instead the inside lights shining on his empty white walls and carpet, the swelling darkness slowly pushing in against the windows from the courtyard. Following his path around a collection of nameless shadows sliding beyond the light from the hallway, he moved along to bedrooms three, four, five, six, passing random bathrooms as he went. Pol Roger bottle in one hand and glass in the other, in spirits rising, Martin's shifting sensations and perceptions sensed an otherworldly slightness. He could hear a distant whisper in this house or perhaps in its surrounds, silent, black and hidden. He wasn't only drunk, he was moving gently, seamlessly, hearing almost no echoes and only a distant, calming murmur.

In each bedroom the radiators were on, the beds fully made, dressing gowns hanging, slippers on bedside mats, tissues and bottled water plus glass on bedside tables and the curtains were drawn against the night. In all the bathrooms there were tasteful shades of fluffy towels in many sizes, electric toothbrushes and toothpaste, along with matching sets of soaps and toiletries. All just for Martin, who would sleep in a different room every night.

Stroking the towels and tiles in every bathroom he sensed the different textures. His fingertips remembered another faraway contrast between soft lukewarm water and the harsh cotton fibres of a friendless towel and an unwelcome touch. A kiss, unexpected, sudden touch. Touch. Let me help you with that.

His Shadowhurst bedrooms were immaculate like posh hotel rooms, but with no bins or televisions. Alison had done a perfect job. The Pol Roger took him by the hand, warming and mildly dizzying, and led him back to the sitting room and the row of chrome and the reddening fire, getting darker and greying to embers. Jazz was playing and as Benny Goodman gave way to Oscar Peterson in the CD shuffle, Martin dozed off into tunnels and pathways, some dark and watery, some wispy aired, and all of them alien.

Morning found him curled up on the sofa and cushions still in his coat and boots, empty glass in hand. His day opened to the sound of knocking, a rattling on the French windows. Peering bleary-eyed and sleepy-confused, he sat up and saw a sharp black silhouette contoured with a halo of bright white morning light.

Standing on the terrace a few minutes before she had knocked, Sheila clocked the clenched glass and the bottle on the floor and was mildly surprised that there was only one empty. Mrs Mainwaring usually sip, sip, sipped her way through at least two bottles of Pinot Grigio of an evening. When she saw Martin sit up and start to stand she opened the unlocked doors and with a fakely cheery 'good morning, sir' stepped a pace into the room and stood behind the bin parade.

'It's Martin, just Martin. What time is it?' He rubbed his head and pushed his hair aside, continuing through a hoovering yawn and reaching into his pocket before he remembered. 'Who are you? What do you want?' he snapped.

'Your new housekeeper. It's half past eight. Sheila. Simon's wife. He told me to come and say hello and sort out the bins. He said Alison wanted me to do for you.'

Martin peered at her, silent and cold, impatient, remembering that this was so and his sister's shock when he'd asked for someone to make the beds and keep the place clean.

Scratching his head again he looked at the floor and said, 'I don't want to see you. I want you to do whatever you do without asking me and without me knowing that you are doing it.

I want all the beds made every day with clean sheets. I want the house perfect every day. Flawless.'

'But, sir…'

'Martin, just Martin, none of the sir. It's quite simple: you come in, you make the beds, sweep, do whatever you do and you leave. I'll leave you instructions if anything else matters and your money every week. That's all. Can you get me some shopping?'

'Yes, Martin,' she said, 'I can.' And that was it, the way he wanted it, and Alison hadn't even been in the house to help. As Sheila turned away, she said, 'What about the bins? And how do I make sure you don't see me?'

The woman had a point. 'You can come in the mornings starting Monday, from eight to ten every day except weekends. I'll keep out of your way, and if I do see you it will be because I want to tell you something or ask you something – or something. Okay? And don't worry about the bins.'

Sheila nodded and took the cash and a set of house keys from Martin's shaking outstretched hand. 'Is there a list?'

Martin could feel his phone trembling in his pocket and turned his back. Over his shoulder he said, almost in desperation, 'Wait. I want some bread and a pastry, some coffee.'

'I'll have it sorted in the kitchen in twenty minutes,' she said and twenty minutes later, his body quivering for nicotine, Martin was dipping an almond croissant into a large cup of oily black coffee. As he sucked in the caffeine and pastry sugars, Alison, he thought, you told her. Sheila was gone. But there was a message from Joshua. He would be there soon, bringing more spare keys, some bottles of amazing red wine and a couple of DVDs for them to watch. Shivering slightly over his coffee, mouth working around his pastry, Martin stared blankly at the floor remembering, broken images floating into his noisy brain, fracturing the rhythms, cracking through the fading hiss.

Then he said, spitting buttery flakes and very loud, 'White. I want it painted white.' He sent a hurried text to Joshua. The kitchen windows stared blankly back and outside an excitable blackbird was screaming, its message shrill and alarmed. A gloss of black and yellow. It's you, it's you.

Later, half dozing on the sofa as Gershwin's 'Rhapsody in Blue' pounded the walls, and Leonard Bernstein drove the New York Philharmonic ever harder, Martin was thinking about which bedroom to sleep in. The place was like a hotel, with all the rooms the same except for the master bedroom, which had a dressing room and walk-in wardrobes. Not that. It was the bathroom, the bathroom was too close, and as he drifted in and out of sleep while Bernstein's trombones sawed the air, he saw the bathroom routine. It was the same every time, but only when Alison had gone down the short hall into their bedroom in her fluffy pink slippers and flannelette nighty. 'Alison's a big girl, isn't she, my darling.' And indeed Alison was, always ahead, always on the rails no matter how slippery they got, always in charge, all seeing, all knowing. Except she didn't see this. She never saw this. His mind remembering the steam, the cold tile, then being in the top bunk with the ceiling closing down and Alison telling him 'go to sleep now, Martin, go to sleep' and him counting out loud, complicated sums and long divisions, almost shouting his control until she told him, 'Shush, or Mum will come up.'

Lines

By the time Joshua arrived from town, Martin was showered and changed into clean blacks and sitting on the sofa, music system blasting Meatloaf's *Bat out of Hell*. He didn't notice Joshua come in from the kitchen with a coffee and a village newspaper in hand. Martin got up and started rearranging the dozen bins into a new row, with every other bin some ten centimetres closer to the terrace than its neighbour. It was a slow, precise process so Joshua sat down to observe, patient and calm and enjoying the slow, methodical touch, the precision and, unbidden, the thought 'all will be well'. In the space between tracks he coughed, and when the last bin was in perfect position, Martin stepped back and glanced at Joshua. With a nod he reached into his pocket and back out again, snapping as he dragged his hand through his hair, 'Lunch? Have you eaten?'

It was well past lunchtime and Alison had warned Joshua about the fags. Rather disturbingly for Alison, Martin had made Shadowhurst a smoke-free zone. She didn't understand it and this perplexed her.

Without a smile Joshua pointed out that two out of three ain't bad.

'What? What are you on about?' The track was long over.

'Joke, Martin. The song. "Two out of Three Ain't Bad". It's just you and me, Alison isn't here. No Alison see, just a joke.'

'We're not the bloody Musketeers,' Martin snarled back, staring at him, eyes shifting high speed side to side as he burned a laser line into Joshua's gently smiling gaze. They two stuck eye to eye, absorbing, sharing, waiting for whatever could happen next.

Martin broke first. 'Alison went home yesterday. She said you were coming. So what happens, now that we're here? What's next?'

Joshua, calm and steady on the sofa, the spatulate fingers of his left hand tapping slightly on his left knee crossed elegantly over his right. A couple of gold bangles on his wrist, a strange contrast with his new Derby shoes, glinted in the soft light, their reflections dancing on the chrome. Gazing wayward at the little holes on his shoe and relishing its fringe decoration and soft sandalwood gleam, he was just waiting, savouring the question, the moment, the attention. 'Nothing really. I suppose that's the point. Alison and me, we just want you to feel calm, have a bit of a change, that's all. I guess we hope you'll be okay without the job, the office, you know.'

He picked up the *Sussex Argus,* reading out loud, 'Man Suffers Life-threatening Injuries in Tractor Fall'. The story said that one Julian Nettlesby had fallen off a tractor as it turned too sharply at the end of a field. Leaving Julian Nettlesby flat on his back in a sticky furrow, the tractor had continued randomly on its way. Eventually bouncing to a gentle stop in a hedge, it had stalled. According to a woman walking her dog in the adjacent lane who had 'assisted at the scene', the man was 'smartly dressed and carrying binoculars ... appeared to be intoxicated'. Joshua, confused and wondering if anyone read this stuff, sighed. He was already approaching boredom, except for the entertainment potential of Martin without cigarettes.

He looked up expectantly at Martin and waited some more for an answer to his question.

Martin was tapping an irritating rhythm on the nearest bin with a pencil, and instead repeated his question. 'Lunch? Have you eaten?'

Joshua was staring across an abyss empty of emotion, a canyon whose far-off slopes reached steep and high into an unknown void. Somewhere there in that darkness was Martin. Joshua sighed again. 'No lunch. We've got too much work to do. We'll get something in the village later. There's an ad in here for a tea shop boasting "delicious buns, cakes and light meals"'.

Martin scowled and headed for the fridge. Returning with his mouth full of tuna fish, he mumbled, 'What work? We got all caught up last week.'

Odd response, thought Joshua as he explained, 'It's not much, just stuff about here, the place. I can get the painting underway, but what do you want to do about the rest of it, the gardens, the woods, the sheep? Or do you want Alison and me to just handle it?'

'Okay, okay, okay,' Martin answered through his mouthful of smelly tuna fish, careful not to lose a crumb. 'Just do it. You know what I want, or just do what you want.' As he wiped a grubby finger around the tin to catch up the last tiny morsels, Martin added, 'What do you want?' Joshua dropped his head and through his hot blush mumbled something about cake later.

So cake in mind they sat, with Joshua explaining and Martin considering every option, reducing each to their own binary self, before slowly coming to vague half-hearted decisions. The gardens, 'weed them and mow things'; the woods, 'don't know, it's just trees'; the sheep, 'black ones and white ones, one for every 300 square metres'. Together later with their cake,

Martin counted crumbs and calculated how many bits of mixed fruit were in the slices of fruitcake and watched as Joshua gazed around the tea shop unaware that he was observed by other takers of tea, intrigued by his flawless rural glamour. Had he known he was under view he might have blushed and placed a careful hand on the knot of his perfectly straight tie.

'Seventy-two and 239,' said Martin conversationally. 'All irregular.'

Startled from his reverie, Joshua struggled to focus, so used was he to Martin's long silences. He had been unexpectedly lost in the pale green coolness of the room's walls, strangely comforted by the excessive floral decor, the soft murmur of subdued conversations and the distant tinklings of cutlery. He heard Martin say, 'It's weird this, this cake and no fags, being in a place like this. Never done it before. It's just weird.' And he crammed in another piece of cake, not counting the crumbs as they fell or how many bits of mixed fruit were left. Joshua sipped his tea, watching the cake get gobbled up and smiling as Martin reached for another slice. Impenetrable and yet maybe clearing, that canyon's fading dark.

***

Since starting work some ten or so years previously, Martin Cox had never taken a day off, had a holiday or barely deviated from his daily routine. Even after both parents died, his pattern remained the same. He stayed on his daily Morden to Putney route, dogged and determined that nothing was any different, at least not for him. But then he had to move away from the rotting debris of a three-bed semi and into his posh flat next to the park. Joshua had found it and Alison approved of it. But when Martin finally accepted that he had to move, it was on condition that Joshua meet him every morning, that he be there out on the pavement in front of Martin's building. He had to travel with Martin from the flat, so that Martin got to the 93 bus stop at Putney Bridge at the usual time. The conversation had started badly.

Standing in his immaculate office, walled in with scientific treatises and law books, Joshua watched in amazement as Martin headed for panic and near meltdown, when they talked about the new flat. They had already discussed in depth how Martin could no longer live in the old place. Joshua had explained that the house must be sold and that Martin needed to move. He had explained that he had found the perfect place for him, a place in town, a place on one floor, easy.

Their conversation about the flat had started quite innocuously, with details of the location, the layout, its size, and Martin had quietly nodded. 'Yes, I know. It's fine. Did you tell Alison? Yeah, should be fine. Take down all the walls, though. I don't want any walls.'

The meltdown came a little later when Joshua, clipping his briefcase shut on the signed papers, forgot himself for a moment and casually said, 'You'll be quicker getting to work from there.' Martin, half listening, answered, 'I know. I know', and then stared at Joshua's briefcase and pinched the bridge of his nose, eyes closed and fighting the buzz and shimmer rising behind them as the notional snapped into the absolute.

Fidgeting across the office, pacing the floor and turning at right angles, like a hovering fly, following an unseen catacomb path struggling to find a way out. Alarmed, Joshua could see the panic and tried to sound offhand when he said, 'You've already worked this out, though. Haven't you?' As the words hit the air Joshua knew that no, Martin hadn't already worked this out. Joshua hesitated, waiting and watching the right-angled march around the room become a single line of steps back and forth, back and forth. Martin paced with increased agitation, alternately tapping at the leather desktop of Joshua's immense oak desk and flicking alternate index fingers at a specific red triangle on the Tiffany standard lamp on the other side of the room. Precision and ping as the hair swung out wild with every turn. As he watched Martin stalking back and forth Joshua was aware that many brass handles, one for each of the desk's drawers, were jingling happily together as the taps on the desk got harder and the paces across the floor got faster.

Martin knowing it, knowing it's what he agreed to, knowing it was all changing, was really changing, a world was slipping away. And it was taking him with it, at least a part, not all but a part. Adrenaline seeping rapidly cell to cell as the realisation and terror rose up and claimed him. 'I can't do it. I can't. It's too complicated, it won't work…', he blurted, his steps shorter and quicker. 'I need to get another place, somewhere else, somewhere.' Back and forth, back and forth, his stride stretching longer again, taut. 'I don't know the journey. I don't know, I've never done it. I don't know… I can't.' His coat and hair swinging and beating the air with agitation rising, sweeping, smooth and fluid in rhythm.

Joshua observed the motion, heard the desktop taps, the pings on the glass and the jiggling brass. The combination was almost balletic. Now, for the first time ever, Joshua saw those ice-cold eyes round and frantic, the intense stare no longer constant, calculated, the eyes instead darting rapidly from side to side, fear flashing, sparking electric and violent. Joshua, his voice soothing and calm, mouthing barely noticed, deeply inadequate reassurances. 'It'll be fine, once you get to know the way. I'll help you. Don't worry. It will be under control and you can always cab it if it gets too much.'

Martin dagger-looked back unconvinced, pulling at his dark hair, holding it tight, his other fist clenched suddenly white and hard, on the edge of being raised. Cigarette ash drifted slow and relaxed from his raised hand towards the floor. It reminded Joshua of fairy dust sprinkled on a hapless innocent who longed to fly. And then suddenly Martin Cox, unsoothed and unreconciled, was still and inspired. His face lost its contortions and took on a look of hope. 'You can help me… you come with me until I get the hang of it. That would work, wouldn't it, especially if you were working only for me and had no other clients.' This last with a certain slyness in his tone – he knew this – and he added, 'You'd have nothing else to do.' The ash sliding down his shoulder and away, a curious anointment, was absolving Martin.

'What? How would that work? I'm a partner, I can't just leave the firm.' Now Joshua was the one stressed, with unanticipated fear making a tour of his senses.

Calm and secure and seeing new lines being drawn, new definitions, it was Martin Cox's turn to sigh and stare. He looked Joshua up and down, flicked at his hair and with his usual composure regained said, 'You resign from the day to day and just go in once a week or something. Tell them it's like some sort of early retirement. You can do it. You know you can and you know I can make it work. That way you can help me to keep on working. It's what I need. You know it.'

So, for the sake of an unknown bus route, Joshua Fothergill started working exclusively for Martin Cox, moving from legal and financial advisor to be his business manager and general counsel. He took care to keep his distance for both of them. The first order of business was the parental wills or rather the lack of them. Once Martin was at the 93 bus top at Putney Bridge and counting his way to the office, Joshua returned to his new home office to deal with the forms, procedures and notifications, as well as Martin's other affairs. Joshua had helped Alison to organise the funerals so this was just an extension, necessary paperwork that neither sibling was interested in. Martin instead stayed buried in black-and-white lines, mark-

ing his empty and his ink-filled spaces in immaculate monochromes.

***

His mother had died first, her disease moving with astonishing speed and killing her within weeks of being diagnosed. She
had been coughing for years, but no one paid much attention
to it. It was just part of what she did, a persistent soundtrack in
Martin's life echoed in sometime stereo by his dad, whose lungs
were probably equally putrid and destined to fail, except that he
died before disease could claim him. Between the two deaths
was a mere two months and in those interim weeks Martin's
father continued to drive his cab every day, evenings too sometimes, and Martin continued to catch the bus and go to work.
Daily he counted the lines in the pavement and then drew lines
and curves of his own from nine to five. Life was a defined
pattern: safe, silent, without desires or emotion, or intrusion or
touch, with nothing of himself available, nothing visible and
nothing raw. And now no fear.

When Martin was alone with his dad in the house, the television was always on loud and its noise became their shared habi-
tat where nothing was unreal, everything was truth and the
soundscapes were all encompassing. They ate takeaways and
never cleared up the mess, a gradual accumulation of filth coa-
lescing all around them, a pathetic incidental cocoon building
up to keep the world away and keep the engine of the ordinary
running with its own momentum. Denial and release running
smooth and true. No shock, no tears, no horror or disbelief
when the hospital called. Nothing was allowed to reach down
into their private abyss and the squalor held out some vague
hope that nothing had changed. They could not do as she had
done and clean it up. They could only eat and smoke and stare
ahead in their television jail, clinging to a familiar status quo.
Perhaps she would come back soon, and then the bins would

be emptied and the takeaway boxes cleared away. But perhaps not. Let's say not.

His parents never knew about Martin's money or how he had got it. He never said, never shared or confided. All they ever knew of Martin was that in all those years since he started work their peculiar son had stayed living at home, reliably giving them most of his pay to cover room and board. He kept back his bus fare and enough for the tuna fish sandwiches he bought every day from the Sunny Sandwich Bar in Putney High Street. They had been able to go on holiday for the first time in years. Cornwall mostly, in the cab, and staying every year in the same B&B in Falmouth. A view of the harbour, walks in the rain and their afternoons sitting smoking in the pub reading the *Daily Express* after a ploughman's and a couple of pints, sometimes a sherry or a port and lemon. Martin's parents had been relieved that he had never gone with them on holiday, although his mother sometimes wished he would even though she knew it would have been unwise. They weren't particularly puzzled that he still seemed to have no friends or companions or that he rarely went out in the evenings, even as he grew older. When he did go out, it was always somewhere on the 93 bus route, always in the direction of Putney and always shortly after he arrived home from work. They put it down to his need for repetition, an annoying habit that his mother's persistent attentions had failed to break. 'Let me help you.' And her own denial.

His father, slightly less irritated by his son's curious obsessions and routines, often worked nights to always be sure to be in the vicinity of the wine bar in Wimbledon High Street he knew Martin occasionally went to late in the evening. When he did go it was likely that he staggered out of it in the arms of a stranger, shouting random abuse, frustrated, angry, tears in his wide, wild eyes, another thing his father didn't get. But he understood Martin's sudden sorrow when he saw his father waiting for him, the disappointment, the trap. Once it was a champagne bar near St Pancras station where Martin had been picked up by the police and his father had had to collect him. How Martin had ended up there his father never found out. The police had been understanding. Martin had been sick in the back of the cab and cried the whole way home.

After his father died Martin stayed in the family house, doubly bereaved, doubly blessed in loneliness and filth, daily going out to work, nightly eating takeaways and watching television flickers, as if his dad were still there and would be home later. He washed in the kitchen and ironed his grubby shirts only on the front and around the cuffs and never took off his jacket at work. Evenings in front of the television, takeaways and Marlboros to hand. Day by day, week by week and no visits to Wimbledon or St Pancras. No point. They were unnecessary journeys. Instead he lay in his bed looking at the ceiling and remembering the touch of a stranger's hand, and he touched and touched and touched again, the stroke soft and the warmth gently rising, and the closed eyes and a moan, and a memory of that stranger's hand holding him, no kisses. He pictured the darkness and rain splattering black in the surrounding trees. He heard the traffic slicing wet through the night. He saw a head thrown back, a grimace, anxious gasps. His own grasp tightened and rapid, his fingertips moving, moving in the dark before his own sudden sharp light. Breath and spirit fell from twisted fetters, warm and wet in his slowing hand, and there were tears in his eyes.

Alison came to call on a rain-slicked Saturday when clouds edged in glinting chromium were pushing across the sky. He was still in bed, counting the silverfish as they crossed the windowsill and the flies rising towards the middle of the ceiling, turning endless lazy angles side to side, back and forth, up and down.

It was Martin's birthday and Alison wanted to take him out to lunch. It had been only a fortnight since their father's funeral, the last time Alison had seen her brother. When he opened the door, naked but for a veil of porous cigarette smoke, he saw her horror and understood that things would change. With Alison taking charge of his life, it would be the end of living at 151 Glenkiln Drive. His only option had been to insist that Joshua Fothergill be consulted. 'Joshua, let Joshua find me somewhere else,' he had said when Alison told him they would be putting the house on the market. 'Otherwise, Martin, you will never move on.' Move on? Moving on wasn't something Martin had ever considered. He didn't know how or why he should, and if Alison knew she never let on. Everything was fine as it was. Martin's world was just fine, just him alone, drawing his same lines, counting corners, cracks and canyons in the sky, keeping the static down, untouched and unwavering. Follow the lines until they brought him back again, back without the fear, without the noise. Endlessly forwards and back in the same safe and uninterrupted patterns.

Alison's staccato piercing the air: 'Martin, this is no good. No good at all. It's lunchtime and it's your birthday. We're going out, remember. And we've got to discuss things.'

He stood there bare and cold, one hand holding the front door and the other his cigarette. 'I know, I know. But why today?'

'Because today's your birthday, so go and get dressed.' Alison picked up the pile of post and found the one from the estate agent, confirming that the house was on the market. It was just a matter of time. A letter from Joshua confirmed the conveyancing solicitors and explained the probate process and that their parents' meagre estate would be split between the two of them, as expected. Alison hadn't seen Joshua either since the funeral, and the letter's facts and figures clicked the lock on those events. She hadn't been close to either of her parents. Their parenting had been functional, dutiful, and she had been a functional, dutiful daughter. Love had not been part of the equation, nor had laughter. Her ambition to be beyond their world had been undiminished throughout her childhood and adolescence. In her parents' front room their traces were invisible, lost amongst Martin's snug squalor. It had only been two weeks since Alison had sent in the cleaning crew to clear up the previous mess. Sighing, she glanced back at Joshua's letter and the dainty curls of his signature, a beckoning tease for her response.

The little house sold within weeks and on the day its contents were removed to oblivion and the new people were due to move in, Joshua came in a cab to take Martin to his new flat. It was near St Pancras with a view of the park. Joshua and Alison had had it decorated entirely in black and white: white on all surfaces and all furnishings black. No walls. A small desk faced the park and a huge television dominated the space. They had no idea how else he wanted it. Neither did Martin really. They included plenty of takeaway menus, taxi services and a map.

Bigwell, Edwards & Staines

After a few days at Shadowhurst, Martin returned, in almost junkie-fix desperation, to his high-priced London hovel. His journey back had been as anxious as the journey down to the country, even with Joshua at his side, mumbling directions and vaguely waving. But the experience had been marginally less fraught and much shorter than the 106 miles the outbound trip had taken. Joshua dropped Martin off and then went on with the Ferrari to park it, with an airy promise, 'I'll see you later. We'll have stuff to go through, you know.'

Opening the front door, hands shaking and sweat blistering in the small of his back, Martin leaned forwards into a familiar lusty embrace. Blended with the stink of empty tuna fish tins and dead Pol Roger bottles was the scent of stale and grubby clothes, and semen-stained sheets left long unwashed. Pol Roger because he'd once seen a display in an off-licence window and liked the name. Tinned tuna fish because it's the pure form of his Sunny Sandwich Bar lunches and he always wants it very cold. Cartons of cigarettes in the freezer. Alison makes sure the place is fully stocked whenever she comes up to town, which is often. She empties the overflowing rubbish. Every once in a while she guts the place, sending Martin to stay in a hotel in Putney for a few days. But the journey is too short, too stressful even with his iPod and My Chemical Romance screaming, so it's rare that he goes along with the hotel plan. It's only because Martin's flat is up so high that there are no rats. Plenty of other wildlife, including silverfish and cockroaches, were in residence. Recently, carpet beetles, persistent in their greed, had been working their way through Martin's carpet. He enjoys monitoring their systematic, spreading patterns.

A soft and slow swarm of familiar and comforting odours reached across the flat's massive open space. Nothing slowed the congregation's lazy progress as it meandered along in the gentle drift of rising and falling air, a muffled, conversational welcome. Apart from the bathroom, Martin's London penthouse flat has no internal walls. There is a kitchenette at one end, the bathroom in one corner and outside two wide balconies run along the exterior walls, meeting in a right angle. Windows and double doors on each side open out onto the terrace, where there is nothing except a grubby edging of old cigarette ends and sludgy black dirt, and the occasional manky feather stuck fast in the grime and grit. Martin never noticed the gorgeous view or that, beyond the London skyline, the gleaming stratosphere stretched up in perpetual and boundless salutation. He never noticed the greeting, welcoming him home.

The unobstructed 160-square-metre flat gave Martin a permanently clear view of his space. There was nothing to suspect, doubt, question or hide from. He could see everything in his black-and-white room, and he could see where it ended, where lines met, where curves mirrored and shifted into other shapes and different shapes in black and white. With expansive views of Regent's Park and Marylebone High Street a short stroll away, his flat was probably the largest bedsit in London, but that had never occurred to him. Black jeans and tee shirts were hanging in the wardrobe, black underwear and socks were in the drawers. Over this black base Martin drapes occasional curiosities: a heavy knitted sweater from Peru, the sumptuous velvet coats, a full-length goatskin waistcoat reaching down to his knees. If he was any shorter the waistcoat would have made him look like a glove puppet. And in each of the six bedrooms at Shadowhurst is the same collection.

Still at the front door, Martin stood quiet for a moment readjusting, greeting his familiars, calculating, swallowing in the scents and stench and lit a stale cigarette pulled from the neglected pack still deep in his pocket. He kicked at the heap of newspapers, leaflets and letters before opening all the windows and the French doors to the terrace. It made little difference to the fug and the contrast between the stagnant, stinking interior and the London air bouncing wild and alive on the terrace confused him, so he shut the doors and windows again. Shaken by tar sticky coughs he stared through the glass at the silenced park, crowded with walkers, runners, people pushing baby buggies, tourists with their silly uniforms of backpacks and cameras and trainers, peering at maps, anxious and confused. He could see their noiseless befuddlement, their curious commitment to being not really lost, but rather stranded and afloat on the endless waves of London's everlasting romance. He saw their shimmering excitement, players on an alien stage where all the props are available and yet barely within reach. He turned his back on all the confusing choices his mind was parading on their behalf.

Coffee ready, fresh cigarettes from the carton in the freezer and the heating on, with his back to the view, he dumped the post on his desk and sat down. The warmth enhanced the torpid aromas and Martin, comforted, knew he was in safe and familiar hands. No noise, no static buzz, no complex demands, or decisions or efforts to inhabit were required. No invasions. He set out careful piles of all the printed matter that had arrived while he had been gone. Newspapers, plastic-covered magazines, junk mail leaflets, investment statements, bills and demands gazing blank from window envelopes, cheques he could almost smell and letters. All were categorised, tidily arranged, neatly aligned.

He opened only the letters, and, smoothing each one flat, he took a large pair of pinking shears and cut their empty envelopes into perfect halves, one at a time. Each rectangular half added to a rising pile was its own collection of sharp right angles, large and small. Martin placed the envelope halves precisely, corners aligned, and put the stack to one side at the edge of his desk. He started reading through the letters. Mostly they were related to his work and money, the stuff that had become his new reality. Occasionally, there was something from Alison or some acquaintance who had got to know him well enough to understand that email and social media didn't work. Those created echoes of static, of noise, so although he read them, he never replied. More rectangles were clipped to size and added to the stack.

One of the letters he did not ignore or cut up was from his boss, with a P45 and his final salary cheque. It told Martin Cox how much he was paid, how much tax and National Insurance had been deducted and the balance, and the accompanying note recommended that he talk to Joshua about it. His boss also wrote that Martin was missed and confirmed that he could have his old desk, as requested. 'Just let me know when to expect you,' the letter said. It was dated a few days earlier. A quick text to Joshua and it was done. Martin knew that the desk would be in his glass room at Shadowhurst by the time he went back. That desk, his desk, his connection, his beginning, his link, an anchor line reaching behind and ahead to his new, quiet but unmapped life.

The desk had been one of the oldest in the place when at sixteen Martin Cox had started first as a clerk and then as a tracer in the offices of Bigwell, Edwards & Staines. His parents had been shocked when he said he wanted to get a job and skip university, but only in that clichéd, conventional way that parents of seriously bright children are expected to be. Eleven A*s at GCSE and Rutlish School pushing him to do the Oxbridge exam. He remembered the excitement when the results came in. His mum's normally blank face showed signs of surprise and slight confusion. Over the washing-up she was pretending to be disengaged, but she heard his dad's joy and swelling pride as he read out the results. He was doing it completely at random in his excitement: 'physics A*, biology A*, two sorts of maths A*, both the Englishes A*, economics A*, engineering A*, politics A* ... yes!! ... ICT A*, design and technology A*.' He was smiling his widest and most sturdy smile while Martin just stared down at his shoes, leaning on the kitchen counter and pulling his hand through his hair. 'That's all right, then, that's done.' He always remembered saying that and thinking it would be enough. Of course it wasn't. How could it be?

He looked up and stared at his father's sunshining face and knew that it definitely couldn't be enough for him, not even close. He looked at his mother, her slightly tensed eyebrows, the greying lines fraying her face, as she coughed and continued resolute and methodical with the washing-up. Maybe it was just enough for her, though he knew she didn't really care as much as his dad did. But he knew she wanted him to stay at home for his A levels and even when he went to university. He knew she would always want him to stay.

On the other side of the room and sliding further and further away from him, his parents faded into abstracted versions of themselves, tiny, weeny creatures far distant from Martin. Martin wondered who he was now. Now he was anonymous and no longer about the eleven GCSE subjects and going for the eleven A*s. Could she still touch him? Could it still matter when she said, 'Here, let me help you with that?' That identity was done with, it wasn't his anymore. Except. And the buzz in his head with rising frequency and intensity, a high-pitched and amplifying scream. The GCSEs had been about someone else, someone whose existence was past. They were Alison's not his, they had been her path, the lesson and the route she had taught their parents. But they should understand that for Martin this was not about a beginning, it was about an ending. The ending marked the start of unwritten space before something else that was for Martin in this moment unwritable. The study, the brilliance, the expectation, the anxiety, the sense of being owned were all over. And just as over had to be the fear, the trepidation, the caution. He could no longer see only their ordinary world or the scope of the eleven subjects and the fixed routine of school, homework, exams, more exams, more homework, more routine, more caution. It was all just someone else's useless furniture and now it cluttered and clogged his tired and teeming mind.

He pasted in place an empty smile for his parents and tried again. 'It's good, it's over, so I'm... I'm done.' The tone was hard, resolute, determined. This was no query and there was no search or request in his voice, nothing that sought their acceptance or their endorsement. It was fixed. His mother turned to face him, sighed and dried her hands, quietly, thoroughly, right down to the gaps between her sterile, red fingers. Turning slightly to reach for her cigarettes and with a quick glance at her husband, she asked Martin: 'So what next? What do you want to do now?' He glimpsed that glorious open vista of nothingness, nothingness he could fill with more nothingness.

He sat down at the kitchen table and with his hands flat, fingers spread firm and straight in front of him, leaned slightly forward and said from behind his hair: 'I'm going to get a job in an office. Be part of the proletariat. I want to labour and toil and be useful and not have to think about anything.' His father was angry and proud and speechless all at once. He had no lecture at the ready, no nugget from Lenin or Marx. No droning on about the abased and downtrodden and the backwardness of capitalism. He offered only silence and incomprehension and annoyance, his wordless mouth working, his head wobbling from side to side. Martin could hear the returning hiss and quiver, seeing slow through his rippling vision as his head continued to pound. He tried combat, adding loudly, 'I've just had enough of school. I don't want to do it anymore. I know what it is and I've had enough. I'm done. I just want to work in an office.' It was the extraordinariness of an ordinary life that called him, a sly siren he wanted to make his own.

Martin saw their confusion, at opposites, anger and patience, red-faced fury and a soft, resigned smile as she twisted her thin gold band on its chapped finger. He would stay home, then. She smiled a secret smile and looked aside at an empty wall. She reached out to touch his hair and as he pulled away and stared at the floor, she said, 'If that's what you want, you just do it.' His father finally found words to say, 'But what about uni, what about trying for Oxford or Cambridge, what about these grades? You've got so far', smacking at the letter with the back of his hand, beating an angry percussive beat. And Martin stared at neither of them nor at the floor but straight ahead and said, 'It's not what I want. I won't do it. I can't do it. I won't.' And they, stock still and silent, unsure what to do next, looked at each other as strangers, blank and slightly afraid.

It was the end of the conversation. He never went back to school, never saw any of the teachers, never shared the excitement of the results, never cared, never wavered, never doubted, never once looked over his shoulder at the super-clever boy with a head full of data and other people's ideas and opinions as he faded from view. His choice, his own choice, steadied his mind, some sort of quiet, easy vacancy, devoid of neutered facts, queries, equations, and even the lasting attractions between atoms that once so beguiled him. His decision, blurted out of nowhere, an action put to no particular thought, made quiet the distant rising road and he saw in the shadows a void of silence as it stretched and beckoned ahead tempting and inviting, so comforting, so other, so softly grey, an anticipation, a tangible gained. And as they two turned away and the white noise started to recede, the radio spat into the air, black-and-white crackles that in his anticipation he did not hear.

***

Looking for a job had been novel. The thrill of reading through the situations vacant ads in the paper had made him wonder how long it would be before they would all disappear from print. Classifieds, display ads, news, features, telly listings, all of it, it should soon be burning holes and craters across the internet to reside online. His mother had sat duty-bound in anticipation beside him, wondering and smoking, wondering and waiting, watching him circle any ad with a certain distant and invisible word. Martin's twitching fingers in his hair and grasping at the pencil to make another circle and put it down again. She sees him as an extension, a still unbroken connection she's allowed to control. You are the one.

And you cough a little and watch and wonder what's in that head of his, what's he thinking, what sits in the dark of the churn and simmer behind that tiny smile, that hint of darkening down on your boy's cheek? You notice he is humming slightly. You never noticed humming before. Should you reach out to him? Try again? You sit still, waiting, wondering, and you understand that he will not, cannot, back off from his course. You don't really care, it will keep him close, close in your orbit, close to your touch. You thought you'd done your job. But you understand those tedious lessons of Lenin and Trotsky, the clinging to what never was, of losses and of the sightless courage of the ignorant. They had taught him something unintended. You had taught him something worse. You watch him circling the same word in all the ads he's marking, and you understand that he's circling the words only because they are unfamiliar. As he looks up and asks, 'What's a clerk?' A word from the world of work he has never seen. And you see for a moment that this boy's trust in his taxi-driving dad and his cleaner mother is mostly there and mostly still intact, as long as it's at a distance, so it's all okay, all fine. But it doesn't always stay at a distance, does it, and you can't help yourself, you cannot resist, and now as always you push away what you should own. You know it's a sharp-edged crack, a dangerous flaw that harms him but you say no, where's the harm. And now you look instead at that moment, Martin's moment and the meaninglessness for him of A level results, university, opportunity. You marvel at his patience, his understanding, how you know he sees you, your love, your touch. And his fear. But this you also push aside to understand that for him there is no more purpose. It was only about following what you wanted, to do what his sister had done. To keep the pattern and to keep you away. A levels are over. They were just there for him to do, for you because you said so. Because you said so. And to keep you elsewhere, keep you away. This you know, but this you push aside as well. You understand that he went along the path, following your instructions and expectations, doing as he was told, as he was told. Now he is moving on, away from the tortuous and unsteady push-pull of every thought, every fact, every moment that his brain has been tick tick tocking for. But perhaps not away from you, though you know better. You have to answer him. You have to leave this moment, this brief glimmering glimpse, this narrow window of fleeting, touchless connection. 'I think it's like a helper, a dogsbody, you know, the person who makes the tea and opens the post in an office or a shop maybe?' And as Martin stares back, clickety clack, you understand any vague ambition you might have had for him is meaningless and that he seeks something else, for the inside of his head, for his life. No decisions, no expectations, no questions, only the simple motivation to open the envelopes of letters that are not addressed to him. A proletariat drone with no mind of his own, just emptiness and no choices. The lessons of Lenin and Marx. You've done your duty and it is what it is. He is no longer yours. You can no longer claim him. He has gone.

He reads to you: 'An entry-level vacancy has arisen for an office clerk in our busy drafting office. Main duties general office tasks: managing the post, copying, scanning, archiving and liaising with internal staff. Opportunities for advancement.' You offer him another cup of tea and another chocolate digestive as he starts to write 'Dear Sir...' in a tight and tidy hand.

***

At the job interview, anxious on the chair, Martin Cox was fidgety and faux-smiling twitchy little grins, his eyes alternately staring at the business face across the divide and then down to the floor. He turned his head away completely to consider answers to the questions, counting the ridges in the elaborate skirting boards, the curves in each square of shiny Anaglypta on the walls. His hair, flopping as the questions and answers went back and forth, was much pulled back. Bill Edwards, middle-aged, sandy-coloured and to Martin faceless, was a lifetime away on the other side of the desk. He observed that 'You're very young, you know. How can I be sure you won't just do this job for the rest of the summer, and then bugger off with your eleven A*s to uni?' Martin, suddenly concerned and sincere, needed to explain, to reassure, 'I have to do this job for the rest of my life. It's going to be what I do, I want a simple job, a good job, a job I can do well. I can't go back to school. It isn't good for me. I have to have this job. Let me try. I promise I'll stay.'

Bill Edwards looked down at the list of stellar GCSEs and back to the blue jeans and tee shirt, the overlong slick of shiny black hair, the fidgeting, the intense, glacial gaze. Then he looked at the pile of also-ran applications. They were all reasonable at the least, even a few graduates in the mix. Yet are any of them likely to have this watchful intensity, the stare, the honest, open eyes, the peculiar need, a radiating energy reaching out to him, this depth of commitment, this passion. There was no other decision he could make, nor even consider.

And so it was that Martin Cox joined Bigwell, Edwards & Staines as an entry-level clerk. He caught the 93 bus every morning from Morden to Putney Bridge and daily counted the bus stops, the people who got on and off and where, the number of men, women, black, brown, grey, white, the school uniforms, the frail, fragile and injured souls at each stop and how many seats were sat on between the stops. He counted the number of green spaces they passed and the number of traffic lights that were green or that brought the bus to a halt because they were red. And then when he walked to the office, stepping over pavement cracks, broken gutters and drains, counting their lines and manholes round and square, he could vary the route daily for an infinity of numbers and calculations. He stored the accumulated numbers he constructed into complex equations and geometric figures. They sat still and neat and tidy in his head until he arrived at the office, where they faded amidst the trivia of other people and their senseless tangles, the links and chains of worlds he was passing through but did not

inhabit. The people good morninged each other and sometimes said 'goodnight' or the occasional 'have a good weekend'
to Martin, but little else.

Martin was very happy that his colleagues ignored him
pretty much completely and that he could be anonymous, faceless. It seemed to him that they spoke to him only in mono-
syllables, except when they gave him instructions for tracing
or asked for tea and coffee or told him to book taxis for clients
or hang up their coats. The office had a view of the River
Thames but he never looked at it, as it slid slowly away towards
some distant unknown. He always looked down at the floor
when moving about the office, holding back his hair, head in
his hand. The floor was unchanging, and the number of carpet
tiles and right angles was always the same. The table legs lined
up undisturbed along the floor. Between the office desks and
the wide windows with the river beyond they stood guard, singular and unvarying.

By all these things was Martin's life measured, organised and
monotonous. He could be quiet and untroubled in a steady
whelm of details, drawings, in black ink on white paper,
counting mouse drags and clicks, finding and defining binary
spaces. Slowly, the clamouring facts bouncing around his brain
were finding order in monochromes and the slow beat of reliable, unpressured repetition. He knew that he was irrelevant
but he also knew that he was trusted, predictable, as his world
was trusted, predictable. Safely detached in his own reality he
could be anonymous, untouchable. Conversations didn't occur
beyond what he understood. He had no need to share anything
of Martin with colleagues for whom he was just a bit too weird,
obviously clever, but a bit too weird even so. Nor did he need
to share the data he carried in his head, but which they could
not possibly have ever understood. And yet after a couple of
years of steady routine and replay and isolation, unseen Mar-

tin Cox was slowly moving, expanding the realm in his mind, growing and progressing from office boy to copying and tracing, losing his resistance to doing more, embracing more without noticing it. He started using the computer and was trusted to fetch and file printouts. He still considered himself a clerk and his colleagues still considered him weird. It didn't matter.

Bill Edwards was watching him, observing the subtle process as Martin started to forget himself. The young man fascinated Bill Edwards. Martin's urgent obsessiveness and that beautiful lack of guile was moving slowly beyond innocence. Bill came to understand Martin's need to be in a space of answers and resolution, simplicity, no traps, no touch. When they first met, Bill had been slightly unnerved by the slender, gangling teenage frame and the hard ice-blue in the fixed gaze. Martin had said that all he wanted was to be in an office, to be a clerk. But the boy's astonishing mathematical and analytical skills, his genius for structural calculations, were evident in everything Martin did. The cups of tea were always filled to the exact same level, the boxes of teabags and jars of coffee perfectly aligned, the stray coffee granules carefully placed in tidy rows parallel with the edge of the counter, or in patterns around spots of water and stains. Sometimes they were aligned to the windows, sometimes to the angle of a chair dragged away from a table.

But from the moment he handed Martin his first Rotring pen, Bill had seen the superb hand-to-eye coordination, the richness of his gift for drawing. For Martin his drawing skill was a given, part of the precision and control, protection against all that threatens him, all that robs him. Back then he wanted only other people's ideas to render them perfectly in straight or curved black-and-white lines. With each passing year, Bill had watched Martin's innate ability to draw, pen on paper and later on screen with a mouse, tablet and in software, as it developed. He marvelled at Martin's speed, working out dimensions, scale and structural loads, never using a calculator or asking someone else to check his figures. He didn't need them checked because Martin Cox knew they were always absolutely accurate. And they were.

At first it was just simple stuff. Then Bill Edwards had asked Martin to help with writing the firm's name on a pile of sketches produced and edited in collaboration with another company. He had handed Martin a 0.5 mm Rapidograph and a steel, cork-backed ruler and shown him a sample drawing already marked with the Bigwell, Edwards & Staines name and address. Martin was done within a couple of hours. After that first task he was asked to add more complex details to collaborative work. Then he was asked to transfer comments from meeting notes to drawings. His lines of text were always perfectly proportioned, tightly kerned and aligned, like the coffee granules, their placements exact and regimented. Draft proposal and manufacturing drawings, previously just rough sketches, he turned into works of precision that were almost art, but for their flawlessness. No cracks, no ambiguities, no disinformation to confuse, distract or stimulate the imagination. Only what could be fixed in black and white, only what could be seen. Soon he was interpreting mechanical and structural designs from architectural drafts for his boss, who told Martin to call him Bill. Martin's unique way of seeing expanded his world from tea and coffee to tea and coffee and drafting and design, and Martin barely noticed.

Martin started working with AutoCAD design software and was equally adept at producing digital drawings from rough sketches and linework. He transformed the messiness of preliminary ideas, bringing order and balance described in perfect black lines and curves with his pen and in perfect pixels with his tablet and mouse. Engineers and architects handed over rough drafts to Bigwell, Edwards & Staines, and Bigwell,

Edwards & Staines handed back immaculate renditions completed by hand or later as digitally produced CAD copies printed on digital plotters. Martin was fast too, preparing multiple versions of designs for engineers and architects to review, improving and expanding, totally accurate and serene in the black-and-white binary spaces he was creating. He baffled his parents with tales of houses, engines and patents for secret inventions and yet still refused suggestions of college or university. Instead he took a short night-school class to learn how to draw better.

But Martin's understanding of how to render two-dimensional sources, his economical approach to problem solving, the directness of his style were already beyond what evening classes could offer. His learning was his own process, the learning of a new grammar, a mode of observational drawing, experienced and executed with perfect control, unambivalent and unpolluted in the purity of black-and-white lines. They hold whole worlds, and their mass was exposed and rendered in Martin's tidy Rapidograph lines. For Martin everything in his life could be reduced to binary structures, to untouchable black and white. Every experience or expectation could be defined as something pure in an algorithm or applied in software. Calm came when he could see the code, decipher it or compound it. He might understand that light shows where the shadows are, so he redraws the shadows in lines of black and white.

For Bill Edwards, Martin's only flaw was his obsession with finding what was wrong, imperfections in his idea of balance in a drawing or design. It would bring him to a halt, and he would flatly refuse to continue working on any drawing he considered deficient. If the curve of a banister was sketched with measurements too short to reach between the floors, or an exterior door was placed too high above the ground, Martin rejected the work. For Martin each collection of lines had to be immutable, a series of matchless routes and curves gliding across the page or screen in unblemished grace and mathematical purity. For Bill Edwards it could be extremely tedious. But the upside was that he could trust Martin Cox to point out errors and even to propose alternatives, thereby enhancing the firm's reputation and billings. By stealth Martin Cox's job was turning into what Martin had never intended, but he barely noticed.

Accidental fortunes

As Martin penned crisp and tidy answers in sharp, hard Rotring capitals on his correspondence, he sucked long and deep on his fourth cigarette since coming back to the flat. Dragged deep down from his lungs came a sudden explosion of spit and aged phlegm, festering, dense and hurting. He coughed and rumbled the mess onto the floor, noting as he did that the letter pile was going down. Between sporadic coughing fits he numbered each letter, placing them one at a time in sequence in a box file for later when Joshua arrived. Onto an A4 sheet, he wrote additional associated instructions, comments, numbered to correspond with the numbers on the letters. He opened the rest of the post and, with the exception of the cheques and financial stuff, took his shears and cut all of it into halves and quarters. He piled the array of corners carefully in close alignment on top of the halved envelopes, with the snipped newspapers and magazines last. Those that threatened to topple the pile he dropped onto the floor with the congealing mucus and cigarette ash and ends.

Answering emails was slower, because Martin read every single one, even the rubbish, the crap from the one-night stands who wanted to see him again and those promising to surgically enlarge his penis. The one-night stand messages were bounced with an undeliverable mail address message he had concocted, dragged to the trash and the email address added to an auto delete list, along with those of the spam. Although the first few encounters had been intriguing, Martin had soon tired of the games people wanted to play just to have sex. Dates generally went wrong for Martin and there was often a mess to clean up afterwards. Sometimes money was involved, but mostly the mess was sorted with lovely presents sent by Joshua the next day with some flowers and a gentle note. 'Sorry. It's not you, it's me.' It was mostly true, except for the sorry part. He never wondered why. He didn't care. And Joshua never asked. By the time the next opportunity arose, Martin had forgotten.

Martin was sitting staring at the screen still as a swan and still smoking when Joshua arrived, having parked the car in the secure car park on the Marylebone Road. Joshua wasn't particularly surprised to find Martin smoking again. It was part of the binary pattern, black and white, up and down, life and death, here and there. You and me, he thought, but he said instead, 'It's been a while. What've we got?'

Martin got up and walked towards the opened door and stubbed out his cigarette on the carpet. Turning back to his desk he followed a trail of burn marks and cigarette ends, a familiar track of nicotine cinder paw prints running back and forth from his front door to his desk, and from the desk near the terrace to the kitchen area and to the bathroom. Familiar routes he could follow and count along, they had the added excitement of changing numbers and juxtapositions, especially if the cigarette ends got kicked about. 'Here,' he said, handing the overstuffed box file to Joshua and pushing the stack of rectangles onto the floor.

'How many?' Joshua said and Martin just brushed back his

hair and shot back, tense and on the edge of teasing, 'You know I know and you know I'm right, so what's the point of telling you?' He stared and Joshua sucked at his expensive teeth and toyed momentarily with the idea of pretending to count all the corners. He realised that this would be pointless because Martin already knew how many there were. And now time was slipping, so masking his irritation he said instead, 'Let's just get on with it, shall we, it's getting late.'

Martin said, '262,144', and kicked the pile in the general direction of other similarly cornered debris. He noted with satisfaction the shifting of all the other corners, his numbers making a new shape. His. 6,134,170.

They went methodically through the box file, working together on requests, reports, authorisations, transfers, contract updates and changes. Eventually, they reached the letter from Bill Edwards, close to the bottom. Late London shadows were reaching into the room. In the softness of the light, its pale ambers and its slow burn stretching into the horizon, Joshua was dreaming. Snapping back, he glanced through the letter and sucking at his teeth some more confirmed that 'It's being picked up on Tuesday and taken straight down to the house. If you want to see it on the lorry, Bill would love to see you. We could drive over together if you like.'

Martin pondered a while, remembering Bill and their many journeys, and listened to the hiss and fizz, so much louder than the whispering amber and tangerine light, and could not decide. What would be the point? 'No need. As long as it's at Shadowhurst next week.'

The desk was the only old thing that Martin wanted in the house, apart from his albums and CDs. It was placed as requested in the centre of the glass room, an altar to hours of lines and curves that would now be drawn under rain-washed glass or sunlight shining bright and hot. And letters. Martin writes letters that no one will read. Dear Mum. Answers please. Numbers and dates along the lines, numbers and dates. And beside the black inscriptions, between his drawing and in their spaces his fists clench tight and his knees jig up and down, up and down. Anger, watching the sheep slow-step across the far paddocks and the swans glide on the lake, unimpeded innocents. Thank you, Bill, for sending me my desk. Thank you, Bill, for all the letters you have sent. Thank you, Bill, for not expecting answers. Thank you for not asking.

Once upon a previous life and in another time, a letter from Bill had changed everything. It had changed everything. Turned Martin away. Turned Martin onto a different set of patterns and routings, turned Martin from circles and finite lines to the beginnings of things unfinished. But it was not so very far away.

***

Martin had been with the firm some two or three years or so, following his lines, counting and calculating his way through the days, to-ing and fro-ing on the wheezy bus and walking the same path home. Ignoring his mother, resisting her even, silent, less submissive, less pliant. Yet still that hiss and fizz would rise, his heart pounding in rhythm. The sound of her step treading deliberate and slow up the stairs and along the hall. The coughing in the mornings as he heard her fill the kettle. In these small regularities are patterns made, are cages crafted, weapons honed.

He got home every day at ten past six, would eat his tea, sit in the front room when his dad came home, and they'd stare together at the dancing screen. On the weekends Martin stayed in bed or walked the route of the 93 bus until the end of the line. Leaning over Putney Bridge, the apparent randomness of the river water's movement unsettled him, but he would stare at it until the haphazard, rippling shapes rose to such intensity that he was forced to look away. Sometimes he went to a wine bar in Wimbledon High Street and tried to talk to people who might look like they were as alone as him, but they never were. Sex on Wimbledon Common was easy and convenient, but only when he could cope with the conversation that had to go with it. It was better once he got the hang of the ritual and the sentences were predictable. 'My name's… what's yours?' 'Martin. I only want sex.' And then the look of slight confusion or surprise and occasionally wide-eyed excitement, which was the most convenient response. Hand in cringing hand leaving the wine bar, Martin feeling slightly sleepy with the warmth and the wine but aroused and with a pounding heart. The best place was near the Mere, far enough from the road but quiet and secluded. It was a favourite pattern, rutting in the dark with a stranger, Martin's hands tight around another body, a stranger's fingers pressing hard into his soft flesh, sweat and tears running and a face of tangled anguish and fleeting delirium, as it suddenly is done and calm spreads in a swarm of warmth and tenderness, of Martin's love for his own body and its sublimely innumerate functions. Touch made touchless. Alien and anonymous, helpless and unchosen the words, the breath, the hunger satisfied for a little while. Once done like animals they would turn away and slouch off into their other darknesses, once more alone.

***

And then one day the routine all started to unravel. Something secret and unseen had pulled at the thread and slowly unstitched the delicate patterns of this, Martin's tightly woven life. At work one day: all he had said was 'This is wrong, Bill, I can't do it.' It was an almost random comment, a seemingly inconsequential observation, just like many other times before. But this time there was more that was wrong than just measurements. There was something illogical in the drawing that

Martin didn't understand. He couldn't see the paths in the lines, the places they described, and it was worse than unsettling.

Bill sighed and reminded himself to be patient. 'What do you mean, Martin?' They had been here many times before and the usual routine was an explanation of the mistake and a suggestion to the client to redraw their draft, so that Martin had no ambiguities to resolve. 'Is it the dimensions or the angles, or what?' Bill watched as Martin stared at the wall, lost and baffled and stuck.

'I don't know, I don't even know what it is I'm trying to draw, but it's wrong, there's something missing, and they have to tell us. They have to explain,' he said, his voice rising in pitch and the tempo of his words increasing.

He turned and stared at Bill wide-eyed, almost desperate, the buzz and hiss rising in his head and almost visible, dancing and strobing across their shared space.

Bill picked up the drawing. It looked like so many other routine sketches, illustrations that had to be formally drafted into a series to go along with a patent application. So far so blah. A patent for an inkjet printhead, the notes said, a component for a larger system. But to Martin it was wrong, and tears were filling his eyes and he blurted out, 'I just don't see it, I can't draw it, I need to know what it's for. What they want.'

And Bill, embarrassed at the passion, leaned forward to reach out, but knowing better and drawing back rested his hand on the desk instead. A long, deep sigh, and he said, 'Let's leave it today. We can ring the client and see what we can do. Calm down. It's fine.'

Martin looked out from behind his tears at a wash of colours, concentrating on not letting the teardrops roll in lazy indictment down his upturned face. He held up his head, slightly back, slightly defiant, containing them. 'It's their problem, not mine, I mean ours. I can do it, but only if we have better details. This is incomplete.'

Gruff and suddenly aloof, he turned back to his desk and started drawing precise and quickly a series of overlapping, rotated triangles. In sudden perfection they bloomed and marched across the sheet like algae, as Martin filled them with perfectly spaced lines, back and forth, back and forth, the ink running to keep up with his pen, and shining bright and drying suddenly on the perfect smoothness of the page. Black and white, black and white, and then it was done.

Later, calmer, as he was leaving the office at the end of the day, he passed Bill's open door and Bill was waving at him to hang on as he cradled the phone on his shoulder. Martin heard Bill say: 'Right. Great. We'll see you in the morning. Should be around half nine, depending on the traffic.' He hung up and said to Martin, 'Be outside here tomorrow at seven o'clock and we'll get up to Cambridge to meet with them. Get it all sorted out. All right?' Martin observed the eager enthusiasm, put a cigarette between his teeth, nodded and headed for the 93 and home. Resolved for now.

He told his dad he was going on a business trip to Cambridge with his boss. 'It's about a drawing, that's all.'

'I always knew you'd make it to Cambridge one day,' his dad replied, but Martin didn't get the joke. Instead he stared at the television between counting the baked beans and chips on the plate his mother had put in front of him, and working out their ratios.

'You'll need to be clean and ready early,' she said, wistful hope mingling in the stifling steam of the cramped kitchen.

'I know, Mum. I'll be ready early. I'll catch the first bus. No need to get up for me. I can manage.' And he stared even harder at *Animal Hospital* and creepy Rolf Harris. She stared too. 'He's wonderful, isn't he, and such a clever painter.' Martin filled his mouth with eight chips and twenty-two baked beans and seven millimetres of sausage, then pressed the remote to change the channel.

The next morning, waiting at the bus stop for the first or maybe second 93 bus of the day, Martin felt strangely ready for what he did not know would happen. A sensation of anticipation, but with no noise in his head. Instead he knew that the bus would come, so he started counting the seconds. He knew he would sit upstairs but that he wasn't allowed to smoke there and could calculate the number of puffs he would have to forego for the journey. He knew he would reach Putney Bridge station and be able to dance his unique routine across the lines and corners in the pavement, and that he would have a model in his head that matched their numbers. He knew the office would be closed, and that Bill had said he would be waiting outside for Martin and that they would drive together to Cambridge. But he didn't know anything more, he saw only a blank empty place where something should be. This new rising road not so distant and with shadows still a void of silence, and a new intangible gained.

On the bus and sitting very still in this unfamiliar moment, he was skewered to an unknown shape that he could not recognise. The sensation dwindled away as he counted the lines on the upholstery on the back of the seat in front of him and was reassured that there were as many today as there had been yesterday. The slow shunting movement through the early traffic gradually sent Martin into a doze and he was deep asleep by the time the bus reached the end stop. He woke up confused before he remembered today was different. His path would be the same, but only so far. Walking along the pavement to the office, head down and automatic, Martin saw the unwritten space growing wider and wider, the noise in his head getting louder and louder, biting his lip between the drags on his cigarette as he prepared to step off his map, a surprisingly willing victim of a new unknown.

Bill was shining bright with early morning excitement and waving to him as Martin rounded the corner. 'Ahh, there you are, Martin. All set? We can head off straight away.' A blank 'yes' and a cigarette end dropped into an open drain's wide and greedy gills. It hissed a malevolent dying breath when it touched the fetid water at the bottom. As the car door slammed, Martin was transfixed by the dashboard, its alien colours, circles, needles and lights, an orderly chaos of functions and calculation options. The only car he had ever been in was his dad's black cab, even for his driving test, so the array of dials and switches in this sleek new car held his attention for most of the journey. He counted, calculated dimensions, distances, ratios and fractions in silence all the way to Cambridge. And Bill, glancing occasionally over at his passenger as they burned up the M11, was glad of the peace and appearance of calm. He was also very glad that his clients had agreed to meet them, so that they could explain to Martin what they wanted done and the Bigwell, Edwards & Staines part of the project could be concluded and invoiced. It was also a good chance to show Martin another side of the business, although Bill wasn't too sure what the point of that would really be.

A couple of hours later and they were pulling into a white-lined patch of pavement marked 'Blast Technologies Visitor Parking'.

'We're here, Martin. Time to focus.'

Martin looked about him, unbuckled his seat belt and stood carefully out of the car. 'So this is Cambridge,' he thought. 'Not much to it, not worth the bother of A levels', before turning to follow his boss through a plate-glass door set in grey-clad walls, and into a reception area with a counter and a sign with exchangeable white letters. It said: 'Blast Technologies Wel-

comes Bill Edwards Martin Cox Bigwell, Edwards & Staines.'
'Why?' thought Martin, and he wondered where the students
and the toilets were. 'I need the toilet,' he said as Bill signed the
register on the counter. A smiling lady bobbed up from behind
it and gestured at a wall where there were doors to the toilets.

'Wait,' said Bill, 'I'll come with you.' Smiling nicely back
at the lady as she handed them their health and safety badges,
he followed Martin to the loos. 'Don't forget, Martin, this is a
business meeting. Don't ask for anything, just wait until you
are offered.'

'Okay. But I need to go.'

They were only sitting in the reception for a moment before
two men joined them, making introductions and nodding and
thanking them for coming and would they like a coffee or
some water. The older one was grey-haired, small and stocky,
with carbon-black eyes and a flat, expressionless face that
scanned Martin up and down, top to toe, with almost audible
precision. Martin watched him, cautious and quiet as
instructed. The face came suddenly and unexpectedly alive as
his partner unfolded his long arms to welcome the visitors
like a preacher. The tall, thin co-owner of Blast Technologies
glanced down at his older, smaller partner, looking for a cue.
He saw his partner's teeth appear suddenly from behind generous lips, now upturned on one side, a leer masquerading
as a grin. The lips quickly stretched rubber-band thin into
a charming and beguiling, almost seductive, smile. The eyes
stayed black and expressionless. 'How was your journey? Not
too bad, I hope? Welcome, welcome.' His tall, thin companion's arms were now refolded over his chest and he kept his
stained and ugly teeth hidden. He raised the corners of his
mouth and leaned forward, unravelling his arms again. Shifting
slightly in a half-bow, he echoed 'welcome, welcome'.

Bill, beaming back at the pair, earnestly grasped the outstretched hand. 'So pleased you could take the time to see us,' he said, and gestured to Martin. 'This is the chap who's doing your drafting, and he just wants to go through with you how it is supposed to work.'

With a signal to the receptionist to do the necessaries with teas and coffees, the man with the pictureless eyes and the too-wide smile said, 'Let's go through.' Taking short, rapid steps, he was talking over his shoulder, enthusing about the new design, their hopes for it and how important it was to get it right, so of course they could take time to explain.

'But it's not right,' Martin blurted, confused and over-whelmed and not expecting his voice to sound quite so loud. The words bounced out of his mouth, hitting the walls before tussling with the small group as it moved in an uncomfortable and irregular mess along the pastel corridor. The walls were peppered with images of smiling employees doing worthy deeds between large windows beyond which was a large open-plan office. Martin said it again but this time much less loudly and they all smiled kindly and slightly awkwardly back at him and said, yes, yes, of course. They had to wait until the time was right, until the prescribed rituals had all been followed. As they moved briskly forward towards a large conference room Martin took note of the office cubicles, twenty-four, and the large, airy space beyond the windows looking out onto similar buildings. One less than prime. Subprime. He understood that this Cambridge was an imposter.

In the conference room, Bill folded his long frame neatly into his chair and sat with his elbows on the table and his hands clasped under his chin. Martin was pacing by the window, wanting a smoke before heeding his boss to take a seat. Bill explained that Martin was doing the work for Blast, but that he had some questions. This cue went unheard and the room was filling with a soundless energy, rising as three sets of eyes watched the floppy hair get dragged back and the pale young man fix his own eyes on the ceiling. Still counting the little holes and corners in the ceiling tiles, he squeezed out an almost mumble in his effort not to shout. And he said again, 'I'm not sure what you want, that's all.'

Relief at the broken silence and so they started. 'Let's give you a bit of background, shall we? Blast Technologies has an interesting history and most of the people working here have local connections. We've been working on our technology for a number of years and this latest advance is our biggest gamble yet. We know what we are doing, but this new head changes everything and it could be very big for us. I'm sorry I didn't fully introduce myself. I'm Clive, Clive Marshall, and this is Richard Janes. We're the cofounders of the company.'

Clive's eyes and smile were now both alive and energetic. Richard, mouth still tight shut, was running his finger down his bony nose, bridge to tip, bridge to tip, as he watched his partner in action through beady little pinched-in eyes. Together they nodded across the desk, waiting. And this time, bolder and louder but not in a shout, Martin heard himself say, 'I can't draw your image. I need to understand what it's for because it's all wrong.' The three men stared momentarily at him, hearing that last word spinning in the air, its edgy blades slicing at the vanity of those who think they are in control.

The spin continued in the silence until it was suddenly broken when Bill added that 'Martin's seen something in your sketch that perplexes him. Could you explain more about what it does and how it works?'

Wrong was not a concept to even consider, but Martin still stared blankly at the no longer smiling faces, waiting for what would happen next.

'As I said, let's start with a bit of background,' and standing up, short-but-paunchy Clive clicked alive a screen and launched a thirty-three-slide technical presentation of what an inkjet printhead is, how it works and what it can be used for. Martin interrupted only to confirm his understanding and at the end. He saw that the technology could be used to print onto any surface, from glass and ceramics to clothes and textiles, food and objects even. He understood that the technology already exists and that they use it in homes and offices, but that this was something more.

Warming to the theme and relieved that this curious young man appeared to get it, Richard stopped stroking his nose. He peered through fingerprinted specs at an empty point on the wall and briskly said, 'Eventually, it will do all this as well as working in a desktop printer. But we're a long way yet from that point. We see this as a starting point for the next generation, and a way of changing the production of all sorts of things. All sorts...'

Martin had watched the slides, different ideas appearing and disappearing, storing up questions in his head until they reached the last slide, the one that said 'Questions?' Looking at the prototype they had placed on the desk, he was still wondering why they had designed their printhead as it was and not as it should be. 'It's still not making sense to me, why this is incomplete, based on what you've told us.' Martin continued, 'Fluid flow and droplet size and control could be much more precise, with one small change. And I think you'd need to jet less ink so prints could be cheaper for users, yes?'

At this last observation, Clive and Richard paused open-mouthed and the blood drained from their faces. They stared across the table at the impertinent young man who had seen something hidden, some gem of engineering logic that had passed them by. Martin had stopped short of calling it wrong again, but there was no mistaking the challenge, the defiance. They weren't quite angry, but they glanced one to the other, shocked and disbelieving and uncertain how to respond. They pointed out that they had been designing printheads for the last nine years, and 'with all due respect to you and of course to Bill, I think we know what we're doing'. But Martin, with rising confidence, pulled back his hair and said, 'I don't know how, but you've missed something.'

Neither partner knew what to say, or how to respond. They sat leaning across the table, the carbon eyes and the smudged glasses fixed on Martin. As the sandwiches and fruit were wheeled in for lunch the brittle crystal instant shattered. The atmosphere breathed a little easier, and new air and scents were filling the room.

'Perhaps this is a good place to pause, and we can learn more about how you came up with this idea,' said Bill, while Martin just stared at the prototype, turning it over in his hands, weighing it and peering through a loupe at the print samples scattered about on the table, counting tonal transitions and fascinated that there were no visible lines or patterns.

***

They ate carefully. Clive and Richard alternately glanced sidelong at each other and at their curious visitor. Bill continued to chat, a comfortable stream of trivia swirling around them, washing away the broken shards. Fed and watered, Martin stayed quiet, eyeing up the last of the tuna fish sandwiches and not sure what was supposed to happen next. This place was not Cambridge, but a business just like where he worked, just another business where other people worked, just ordinary, just another cog in the machine. His head was full of ideas, not about what was wrong with the Blast prototype, which would do what they wanted, but with why the design was incomplete, imperfect. 'Why,' he said suddenly, 'why have you made the chamber this way?'

Clive and Richard looked hard at Martin and Clive said,

'Because it's the logical thing to do to improve on what we've done before. Do you have a better idea?' The sarcasm shrouded in an insincere smile as Richard proffered more sandwiches.

Martin, chewing away on another right-angled and crustless tuna fish triangle, stared at him and said through the mush, 'Yes I do. I can see a way to make this printhead much better for what you want it to do. It has to jet fast with minimal energy and it mustn't be prone to clogging. That's what you want, isn't it? What I would suggest is to improve its performance when it's active, especially for what you've said you want it to do. It would be much better and...'

Bill stopped him. 'Martin, are you sure, you really can see a better way?'

'If you can, we'd be interested to know how,' Richard interjected, sarcastic and faithless.

Bill looked carefully from face to face, at the sandwiches, the prototype, the print samples, and remembered a lesson from his father. Don't share your secrets without a deal in place first, he had said. At the time, the conversation was about Christmas presents and if he should tell his brother what he'd got their mum for Christmas. What price the secret, if he shared it? What risk of the secret being spilled?

But Martin was way ahead. This was a business. This was why all those young men and women in their twenty-four cubicles and their view across the open Cambridge skies were there, because of money not study. He got it that Clive and Richard's brilliance didn't extend to a dual cavity input and output system that would provide constant pressure to keep fluids flowing consistently and minimising the risk of clogging. They'd never thought of it before and now there was no room for such a radical departure from what they knew was right. Or what they thought they knew.

Clogging had had a slide all to itself in the presentation, so it must be very important. Martin had his own brilliance to share, and if it was business it would have to come at a price, just as his work for Bill had a price, and Bill's for him. As the quiet descended, a nameless energy rose in the room, creeping up around them, wisping its way across the spaces in between, across the gaps, into their imaginations.

Martin said, 'If I tell you how this can be improved, what will you pay me?'

'Is this a joke?' Clive laughed and leaned back in his chair, hands on head and arms raised bent at the elbows, convict style and man-spreading in supreme confidence. He looked across at his colleague.

Richard, his brain in overdrive and his mouth working desperately around formless, silent sounds, frowned and leaning forward in a contrasting scoliotic hunch peered at Martin and said, 'What do you want if your idea really does make a difference to my design?'

Martin had been thinking £25,000, which was what his dad always said he wanted to be able to spend on them for a year, just for presents and little trips to the countryside and new clothes. But Martin said nothing, instead counting how many times he could go from home to work on the 93 for £25,000, if he didn't get a weekly season ticket but paid his fare every day.

Bill looked in shocked silence from Martin to Clive and to Richard. Clive answered first, licking his lips, irony oozing at the edges of his mouth and almost dribbling down his chin. This was all a silly joke; the boy couldn't possibly have much to add. 'We'd have to discuss the details, but we'd be prepared to offer you a percentage of revenues, if the prototype works. More if your design holds up in the manufacturing process.'

'£25,000...', Martin ventured as Bill cut in, '...would be added to that for me as broker.' Martin, fully off his map and ambling blind across a blank landscape, was trying to calculate what numbers they were really talking about but had no starting point, so he just closed his mouth and eyes and nodded. 'We'll need a contract, like an employment contract that says what we've agreed to do together.'

Bill smiled at the phrase, which was his from three years ago when he had asked Martin to sign his employment contract. He added, 'I can put that in hand and send you over a draft. It will be an agreement in principle, prior to anything formal, but it will be binding.' Rising as he said this, Richard and Clive rose also, smiling at each other.

'And we'll expect the draft for our patent application, when?' Clive said, with just the merest hint of smug.

'When I can show you what it should look like,' Martin said. 'It won't take long, once we've an agreement. You'll probably want to rewrite your application in any case.'

They stopped smiling and looked back in a state of profound confusion, a mixture of fascination, shock and annoyance. Maybe it wasn't all a silly joke.

'Thanks for lunch and your time,' Bill said. 'I think it's fair to say that this has been a quite extraordinary meeting.'

Small smiles and nods and now Clive and Richard were running their fingers through their hair and scratching at anonymous itches. Hands on backs of heads, sidelong glances at Martin and neither of them really sure if they should take him seriously or not, if this was all silly or not.

'Blast Technologies is based on innovation and unconventional approaches to problem solving,' Richard said, not realising that he was quoting from a press release, his brain incapable of coming up with an original closing line.

'Yes,' Martin said, 'and now you can have new problems to solve.'

Another cliché of indeterminate origins. Bill was holding the plate-glass door and shook his head as he thanked their hosts.

Out in the fresh air, he let out a long sigh, and said, 'Well, that was quite a performance. I hope you know what you're on about.'

Martin looked back at him. 'Now I understand why it didn't make sense, it was just wrong and it was only clear once I understood what they wanted it to do. I can see a better way now that I understand, and they can't see it because they've been doing it their way for too long.' He smiled and lit a cigarette, taking a long, deep lungful and watching the smoke slowly spire away as he exhaled, relieved and calm.

Driving back to Martin's 93 bus stop Bill said he would 'earn the twenty-five grand by tomorrow' and so it had been. The next time they were at Blast Technologies it was with a signed and witnessed copy of an agreement in principle, and subject to manufacturing viability, to pay Martin Cox 5 per cent of annual revenues from the Blast PZX26 printhead and its derivatives. He was barely twenty years old. They also had a folder with Martin's modifications to the PZX26, which they had renamed the PZX26C for Cox. The final contract, drawn up by Joshua's firm at Bill's request, included an additional clause that grandfathered the deal in the event that Blast Technologies was taken over by another company. When the agreement was finally signed and sealed, Bill had written to Martin to congratulate him and thank him for getting him the £25,000 brokering fee. When the first commission cheque had arrived, Martin had promptly signed it over to Bill. By the time the second and third cheques had come in and been signed over, Bill had insisted that Joshua Fothergill take care of Martin's financial and tax planning. Martin continued to go to work and quickly moved on from the Blast PZX26C, although he had a picture of it on his wall and occasionally looked at it for flaws, which he never found. Every quarter Martin met with Joshua, who explained what monies had come in and how they'd been invested. There was always the same conversation about what Martin could draw down and about how it was okay to spend the money. Martin's answer was always the same, as they two sat on opposite sides of Joshua's broad and immaculately tidy desk. 'It's fine. I have my pay. And my parents don't want much. I don't need anything extra.' And then Martin's parents had died.

Letters

And once upon a time long since gone, long since away, Martin's dead mother gazed dewy-eyed and said to her husband 'oh look, he's got a little stiffy' and Caroline Cox leaned over to kiss her darling boy, his small fists gripping tight her fingers. 'Who'd have thought it in a baby just a few months old.' And she caressed her son, before leaning over to kiss the stiffy.

'What's a stiffy?' came Alison's slightly rasping voice as she stood in the doorway to watch her parents playing with their son. Alison knew she had to stand at the doorway because her mother had told her that it's important not to get too close to her brother in case he caught her cold. 'He's only a baby, Alison, he's not as strong as you.' She knew that the baby was important, but not as important as her because her mother had told her so. And she knew that what her mother said was always right because her dad said so. He'd told Alison and he'd told her mother, many times, even swearing about it: 'You're always right, aren't you, always bloody right' he had often said to her mum, so Alison knew it was right to believe what her mother told her.

As she stood there watching and waiting for an answer to a question she was already forgetting, her feet were getting cold in her fluffy slippers and her nose was starting to run again. She saw her parents like bookends bolstering the child laid on the bed between them and wondered when it would be time for tea. Alison was hungry and the thought vanquished her question, which they hadn't answered anyway. 'What's for tea? Do I have to have tomato soup again?' And her father picked up the baby as her mother watched with wistful eyes while he wrestled with the nappy and Martin twisted and turned. Her mother came to the door and steered her off towards the stairs, the dark shadows closing behind. 'Tea's on the way, dear, and I think you can probably manage a bit more than soup, eh?' Alison jumped and squeaked, 'Yes, please.'

It was so long ago, a moment in time that Alison never fully remembered and her father wanted to forget, pretend it hadn't happened. If I ignore it, it'll just go away. But it didn't and when Martin's dad protested, his wife would say, 'What harm, eh, what harm a little kiss?' And she was right in a way, except that the little kiss did not settle and remain confined in one loving moment. That little kiss was not the only tiny moment of loving intimacy, of caring for her son, of a dark need satisfied. He's just a little boy, she told herself, what harm, eh, what harm?

Martin was four or five when he started to remember her kisses and her touch, her frowning concern for his silence. His glance became flat and emotionless whenever she called his name. If he touched at his trousers she would say, 'Poor darling, you mustn't, you mustn't do that, it's naughty.' And she would take his hands away. 'Let Mummy rub it better' she would say, her hand under his clothes, rearranging, holding and waiting. Then she would tell him to go and play outside as she sighed and her face flushed red. Martin did as he was told, did as Alison said he should do, do what Mummy says. He did as he was told and stood in their small back garden watching the sky, feeling an alien sensation subside and his body reset.

Martin's mother had signed for the letter that arrived at 151 Glenkiln Drive. When Martin came home that night she asked him what it was and with exquisite and unfamiliar joy he looked out from behind his hair and almost lied to her for the very first time. It was another very different but equally alien sensation. 'It's just something to do with work. Something I need to look at.'

'But why did they send it here, Martin? Why not to the office? And it looks important.'

'Oh, it isn't really, it's just some stuff I have to read. And they sent it here because I am on holiday next week.' The almost lies coming thick and fast and intoxicating, he added, 'I'm not going to be at work. I'm on holiday.'

She stared, reaching out to touch his arm, but he pulled away instinctively, automatically now and she had no means to hold him. 'But, Martin, you never said, you never said you were going away on holiday?'

Such a clever boy. This lie was of her own making: he had never said he was going away on holiday. 'No,' he said. 'I didn't.' And he took the envelope and went up to his room to read the letter, the contract and the guidance notes that his new friend Joshua had provided.

Then, only a handful of years after that first contract had arrived, another letter had come. This time it arrived at the squalid flat with its sumptuous expanse of dirty carpet, the mess and rank stink, the view across the park, and the same two people. They had been following the same routine too. Just like today, Martin had handed Joshua the box file and knocked a stack of corners to the floor. 16,384. Cigarette in hand he had sprawled across his sofa, his knee bent, ankle to thigh, black jeans peppered with dust teeming with microbes and minuscule flakes of ash, his cigaretteless hand clasping his hair tight to his head. But the letter on that day had been about much more than the desk or the original contract. It too was from Bill, and Joshua had read and reread this second letter in silence, his lips slightly mouthing the text, eyes darting along the lines. He finished reading and looked up at Martin, his eyes round, his hand trembling slightly as he cleared and cleared again a desiccated throat.

'Wow, this is one we need to think about.' He looked down again at the page, swallowing, rubbing under his chin with the back of his hand as he felt the sweat patches slowly seeping under his arms. His heart had started to pound and his blood was surging, booming loud and hot in his ears. The slow beetroot flush was spreading and creeping across his skin. With a tingling touch it moved up under his jaw and tickled at his already engorged and simmering ear lobes.

Joshua's hands were now visibly quivering and his hold on the letter tightened as if to stop it floating away, as if to be sure it was really there. He had wanted to wait for Martin to take the lead, but couldn't help but to blurt out, 'My God, they're actually doing it, they're actually selling up. Blast is being acquired.' Stunned and dizziness rising, he looked at Martin staring at the ceiling, vacant, detached. 'And I guess you're being acquired with them. My God. This is incredible. You know what this means, what this means for you?' he had said.

Supine on the sofa, Martin's face was slowly tightening into a frown, his eyes sapphire-hard pushing to black, his cigarette burning, ash dropping. 'Are you sure about the contract? Absolutely certain?' he said, his voice touched with iron.

The reply came rapid fire. 'Don't even think about it. It's rock solid.' Joshua stared steady and hard at Martin, his eyes completely still, his confidence total.

Martin looked back and pulled at his hair. 'Okay, that's it, then. This really is happening.' Martin remembered another such moment, where crystal lines and cracks in the space around him suddenly shattered. A memory of his first meeting with Clive and Richard, when shock and disbelief had exploded into a strange silence, and all because the sandwiches had arrived.

Martin looked up at Joshua and across this new landscape as reality marched slowly into something tangible, a collection of immutable facts.

'Martin, don't worry about the contract, but you've got choices to make. You've got decisions to make, you know. This is a whole other order of magnitude. They'll be putting your printhead into all sorts of devices and you'll still be getting 5 per cent of revenues.'

Rapid-fire sharp shots into the charged silence ripping it to shreds, ripping all of it to shreds. Barely comfortable on the new map, for Martin a whole other geography was waiting to be navigated. Joshua was still talking. '...mainly if you want to exercise the opt-out.' And Martin Cox silent and now staring at the drifting tones of his tar-stained ceiling, as Joshua carried on, intense and simmering with an uncontrollable energy. The rising presence of his voice was pressing at the edges of Martin's every nerve, rat, tat, tat, tat, the voice accelerating from sharp-shooter staccato into a blur of sound. '...you know your only obligation if you don't opt out is to attend one board meeting per year as long as Blast remains autonomous.' And Martin Cox, now shaking slightly, silent still, listened with growing relief as the tide of words became almost incoherent, just waves of noise turning and splashing onto the battered air. The torrent soothed Martin and he could open his eyes and give a tolerable impression of one who is engaged. Eyebrows raised, head nodding gently, mouth making interested shapes as Joshua's words came into tighter focus. '...so it's not much different from what you have to do now. But if Blast doesn't stay autonomous and gets sucked into the buyer corporation – why don't they say who it is – your contract's only about money. The structures you'd have to work with will get disappeared, if they're just buying Blast for its patents and people. Yeah? Do you see?' A wall of words Martin had eased himself to the top of and he saw, he understood and still staring back at Joshua he answered, 'Yes.' And he stubbed his cigarette out on the carpet.

***

Now the two of them trod that letter's legacy. The letter about collecting the desk, the letter about the final pay cheque. All of it had started that day with the very first letter, the one that Martin's mother had signed for unaware of its significance or of how their lives were about to change. With Shadowhurst in Martin's life, as well as the London flat, his whole routine, the entire pattern of his life, was different. Martin would finally stop going to work, stop the good morninging and occasional goodbying. He'd give up the infrequent sojourns into Wimbledon wine bars and long walks on the common in the dark. He'd stop drawing lines, stop finding resolutions in black and white, stop holding onto the chains that bound his crippled identity. But at what cost? Or would there be a prize instead to stop being who he had always been? What would come next? They two sat staring across the room for what seemed like hours before Joshua recovered his grip. 'Right, I'm off. Got a squash game. Fancy joining me?'

Martin raised an eyebrow and lit another cigarette. 'You can tell me about it sometime,' he said.

They stood up and Martin took the letter from Joshua's outstretched hand. 'Yes, what happens next is what we don't know... but I'll tell you and once it's happening you can tell me. And about the squash?' Martin turned his back. Conversation over. Later on the squash court 2–9 down but two games up, Joshua remembered: 'You can tell me about it sometime.' Since when was Martin interested in squash?

Sitting looking out at London's overpainted canvas, its untidy and spontaneous chaos shimmering against the fading sky, Martin was alone. He finished his tuna supper straight from the tin and slowly sipped at the remaining Pol Roger, growing warm, oxidised and stale in the bottom of the glass. Rereading this new letter from Bill he pondered that seeing him might be good, and not just to say thank you for letting him have his old desk. Martin's appreciation of Bill Edwards was much like his appreciation of his dad. Martin just took for granted their trust and care and ignorance. He was his dad's job, his obligation, his proof that teaching the children would make Lenin's seed impossible to uproot. Except it hadn't worked out quite as expected. Bill was another story, but he had unknowingly parented Martin into this new life of his.

***

At Martin's insistence Bill read the addresses at both his parents' funerals. Only Martin, Alison, Joshua and Bill were present, and on the funeral director's recommendation Bill had chosen the reading about the house with many rooms. No one was really listening. He helped Alison and Joshua with all the arrangements. He'd been the one who made sure that Lonnie Donegan singing 'The Party's Over' would be played for their dad, and that there was no music for their mother, at Martin's request. Alison had just gone along with it all, grieving as expected and curiously powerless. Their mother had died of lung cancer and when the handful of funeral and crematorium staff riffed on 'what a shock, surely so unexpected, she was still young', Martin had been reminded again that people are fools, too often inclined to believe in the power of their own clichés. The woman smoked forty a day, what did they expect? His dad had been killed on the road. They'd sent the police to the office and as they stood to one side, Martin heard Bill ask if he minded him being there. 'Why? Why would I care?' Except that the random brutality of the accident was less to be expected. Falling masonry from a church under renovation had smashed flat the cab, standing still and smoking in dusky London traffic. The driver and his fare had died instantly. They didn't know they should beware of falling angels.

***

London's lights never really fade. Outside his flat Martin saw the sky slowly turning orange and considered venturing out for a glass of wine and company. Then he thought again and changed his mind. He slept alone in his filthy round bed, fully clothed and as a cigarette burned to its lonely end on the edge of the mattress, a soft smouldering whispered into silence in the night. The beetles, spiders and microbes appreciated the slide into quiet. Elegant silverfish wiggle and dart, slinking with impunity across the smooth, flat surfaces, fleeing from spiders, hiding from the light. Cockroaches, bolder and gregarious, socialise in the open and Martin sleeps on. The carpet beetles, elegant in black and brown, leave their offspring to munch contently and unseen on Martin's grimy carpets, oblivious to night or day, to black or white, to the shifting tones that come with the sunrise.

Some days later in brittle spring light Joshua and Martin were back at Shadowhurst. Joshua, striding out down towards the lake, was calling back to Martin: 'There's a swan, look, in the rushes, a swan.' Martin's chest was feeling very tight and he was coughing deep and crackled. 'Whose idea was this stupid tour?' Almost vomiting and slipping on the heavy wet grass, his sliding steps left irregular and imperfect lines behind him in the soggy clay. He slithered awkward and cross down towards the lake. Somewhere in GCSE biology he remembered that swans are the heaviest and largest freshwater bird and that they eat underwater plants. And that they mate for life. Apart from a warning hiss they are voiceless. Still wheezing and hacking, gobbing away brown phlegm and feeling too hot, he reached Joshua, falling the last step into him.

Joshua looked at the frown and the pink cheeks, then watched a final few retches as Martin leaned over, his hands on his thighs, his velvet coat muddied at the hem, dampness rising and a splatter of muddy stars on the heavenly blue. Then he felt Martin's hand on his shoulder, a first, watching as a vigorous glob headed for the reeds and Martin got back his breath. His hand still clamped onto Joshua's shoulder Martin panted, 'Where are we going?'

Joshua, leaning slightly into the touch paused a moment, holding onto the fleeting intimacy, warm and unintended in the chill air, their breath a mingled stream and hanging still. 'I will play the swan and die of music,' he said, and suddenly blushing pulled away and stuck his hands as deep as possible into the giant-sized pockets of his new green wool country coat.

Martin stood up straight and shook back his hair. 'Othello V ii 1604' and walked closer to the edge of the lake. 'Where' – he barked and coughed some more, scowling at his steaming breath – 'are we going next?'

A breeze was easing across the water and pale yellow daffodils nodded in tacit agreement to some unspoken secret they shared in the thin light, some hint of another story. Spring was gathering its energies to reach into the arms of a bright green summer waiting beyond view. Joshua, lost in a tangle of simmering sensations, kept his hands deep in the massive pockets and watched as Martin paused. He was waiting at the lake's edge. Changing the subject to move on from arousal to anything else he could think of, he observed uncertainly that 'this coat's brilliant, you know, it's ideal for carrying stuff. Really clever.' His voice quavered slightly and he cleared his throat, feeling his shoulder still imprinted with the lean and warmth of Martin's hand. Back in trivia territory, the conversation could follow a familiar and reliable route. Joshua tried to forget about swans and music, knowing that they meant nothing to Martin, were just another mechanical prompt for a fact he could bandy, a clever response with no communication intent of any kind. And Joshua could not remember when he had felt so sad. All parry no thrust. He joined Martin at the water's edge and together they looked across the slow ripples towards the reeds on the far side of the lake, feeling a slow and distant pulse, a life of sorts. They watched a pair of swans moving gently along the lake's edge, a silent music white against the blackened surface, sending lesser birds skywards in a noisy flap, battering the perfect quiet. The two men stood still watching, Martin's lungs wheezing and whistling, Joshua breathing easily and stomping his feet against the cold.

'What happens next? Where are we going?' Martin said again.

Joshua had no real plan. It was just a walk, just a simple exploration of the territory, and Martin, he knew, was there under sufferance, keen to get back to his black-and-white lines. He turned to look back at the house, brown and ugly apart from a slowly growing patch of white, a ladder pointing to the place where Simon was painting the back wall. It seemed a long way off. Martin was coughing hard again. Something closer would be better. 'What about poking around over there?' he said, bright and breezy, wondering if all this cold fresh air was really such a great idea. He pointed to a derelict heap of stones and brickwork.

'What for? What are we looking for?' was Martin's response, of course.

'We aren't really looking for anything, that's the point. It's what we might find that matters here,' Joshua replied. He set off, following the lake's edge, sinking unexpected steps into the cold mud when he got too close. Its grasp almost irresistible, clammy and dark, whispering desire amidst the suck and slurp and rising waters poaching its surface. Quickly Joshua was moving away from the lake and striding purposeful, confident and bold towards the trees and unknowingly towards the forgotten remnants of someone else's other life.

Martin was unconvinced but followed Joshua's gaze towards the tumbled masonry. Something reached the end of the line there, he pondered. His brain painted a picture of its once clean and tidy rhythms, lost now in a jumbled series of unreconciled irregularities. Martin saw a collection of broken curves, graceless and completely incoherent, and its incoherence disturbed him. But perhaps it was worth a look and they could work out what it had been for. That he didn't know intrigued Martin. An empty space in his noisy brain, small but growing bigger. He could almost feel it and he smiled as he started coughing again. Through his cough he called out, 'Why did you buy that coat? It's too big and the pockets are the wrong size.' Joshua turned and, walking backwards up the slope, slowed his pace to wait. Martin was still struggling to grab from the chill air a useful breath for his whistling and crackling chest, as he paced slowly up the hill to reach him.

'It's for here, it's a country coat, that's why it's green. No idea why the pockets are so big, though. Perhaps they like big pockets in the country.' Martin, coughing less, pondered a moment. 'Pheasant,' he said and continued on up the hill.

'What do you mean?' Joshua was puzzled and not remembering anything being said about pheasant when he had bought this very costly coat up in Rugeley when he was looking into an investment prospect for Martin's growing portfolio. He'd seen the coat in the window of a shop and figured it would be perfect for visiting Martin when he was at Shadowhurst. And it was. Warm, countrified, green.

'What about pheasants?'

'The pockets,' Martin replied. 'They're as big as they are so that you can put pheasants in them once you've shot them dead.'

'So not for a laptop, then,' Joshua joked. Martin was now ahead of him on the slope and paused again, leaning over, his forearms on his thighs coughing more brown-flecked phlegm and spitting it into the mud where it lay putrid, frail of spirit, slowly dying.

'Yes. Clever. A laptop or a tablet.'

When Martin looked up Joshua was staring at the woods, and at a shambles of broken bricks and stone, brambled and blanketed with long-dead undergrowth. Random primroses and forgotten daffodils and violets, shots of colour against the gloom. The question of laptop versus pheasant was forgotten and Martin instead replied, 'I wonder what it used to be.'

'Since when did you wonder about anything?' Joshua shot back and only slightly joking.

As they got closer they could see that what was left was actually more substantial than had appeared from the lake's edge. The flowers outlined what might once have been an edge or a boundary, maybe even a path. Across a width of some three or four metres there was a series of brick arches, some set low in the ground and some rising to a couple of metres. Broken bottles in greens and browns littered a brick floor. To the arches were joined on each side what looked like something that had once been outside walls. Grey slab-like stones, piled in imperfect symmetry with ferns and grasses growing in the cracks between, were thick and solid. Beyond one of the walls there had once been a balustrade, elegantly turned legs, lock-stepped away from the structure, confident, bold and strong before they wobbled in crisis and fell over into the dirt and lay in disarray on the broken brickwork floor. They marked the edge of a walkway, also in pale stone and mostly clear of mud and weeds. A small but continuing stream of water passed along the length of the stones. It constantly cleansed and whitened them before dribbling away down the hill towards the lake, innocent, pure and telling no tales. Ahead, the trees and undergrowth hid most of the view of Martin's driveway, the slivered gleam of red, a menace through the trees. What remained of the derelict folly's roof was tiled in large grey slates, heavy and solid over the stone and brick walls, sheltering an empty space from light and rain and time.

Under the remains of the roof there were some broken chairs and a few boxes. In a corner left long forgotten and forlorn like the rest of the junk was a rusted shut steamer trunk. Spiders had colonised the various boxes, spinning elegant webs across their edges, swathes of grey long since abandoned. No reason for flies to hover here, nor rats or mice to congregate. The space was dead and dark, in lonely contrast to the gaudy colours beyond its broken walls.

'Did you know about this? Does Alison? What is this place?' Martin hissed, his hands fingering the softly flattened cigarettes in his pocket. 'What is it?' he repeated.

Joshua, equally baffled, chose not to suggest immediately that they go back to the house because the rain was coming, and instead said, 'It's okay. I don't know what this place is. It wasn't on any of the property details or inventories. Maybe no one knew about it. Maybe we've found it by mistake. Our own private discovery.'

Martin, indecisive, drawn and tempted to stay in this dirty, untidy place and smoke, looked away at the lake whispering at the bottom of the slope. The swans sailing gently away into the reeds escaped his gaze. He barely heard Joshua's voice seep slowly into his head, where instead whispered murmurs wanted to be heard. 'Anyway, it's a ruin and it's starting to rain on my new coat. It'll be dark soon. Let's go back to the house.'

Old stories

Sheila was peering into a large kettle of simmering marmalade and was very hot under its sticky mist. Radio 2 burbled gently in the background and Richard Thomson was telling her that he's 'seen good girls in bad places'. She hummed along without knowing the tune and scraped away at the bubbling mass of orange peels, one hand clutching the pan with her grubby dishtowel, the other stirring the sweet molten gold, elbow outstretched. Her tiny kitchen was lined with shelves and cupboards, the shelves bearing pots and pans of every description, her own personal and very private library full of her cooking secrets. 'Sew your soul?' she muttered at the radio as a cross-sounding guitar dropped out, and she turned down the sound to better hear what she thought was a knock at the door.

Standing on the threshold, in the soft spring sunshine, Jodi could hear the muffled sounds coming from within, so she waited patiently, anticipating Sheila's non-surprise and wondering how she would be greeted this time. A moment later she knew.

'Well, it's you again, is it?' And standing with her teacloth and hand on the doorframe Sheila smiled broad and welcoming. Another pair of hands in the hops would be welcome.

'Where are you off to this time?' she said, standing aside and ushering her young guest into the sweet, steamy kitchen. Every year it was the same. Jodi came to twiddle hops on her way somewhere else, but she never managed to go on to wherever it was. She returned home instead to turn what she had drawn and sketched on her meagre travels into more finished works. Then she spent all her time in her studio at the top of her parents' house, completing pieces to sell throughout the rest of the year in the Brighton Laines. Over the years Jodi's reputation had slowly grown and the galleries taking her work were increasingly upmarket.

'Not sure. I started from the end of the pier when the sun was coming up and walked it all the way and I'm thinking of heading north. Scotland maybe if the weather holds. Knackered now, though.' Her voice was low and slightly husky and she spoke through lips that seemed to want to smile all the time, with quiet, slightly remote self-assurance and self-belief.

Sheila eyed her guest and smiled. 'Every year a little further on the road, and every year a little less like a vagabond you look. And I bet you don't make it to Scotland this year either.'

Jodi looked at the bubbling marmalade and the rows of jars. 'There's just always so much to see without going far,' she murmured, breathing deep the sweet citrus air. 'And I always seem to forget that. I don't know, maybe I just like the idea of it.'

Sheila thought for a moment and said, 'That's it, it's just the idea of going off exploring. All you need to know is right under your nose, my lady, always was and still is.'

Jodi had been coming to Catsdown to help twiddle hops since she was sixteen. Back then her parents had dropped her off to spend ten days in digs on the farm and draw for her portfolio under Sheila's watchful eye. But every year since she'd dropped out of art college she had made her own way and invariably she stayed with Simon and Sheila. Just as invariably she always carried her own tent and sleeping bag. Always cheerful, ready to chat about nothing, and happy to give away her sketches, Jodi was popular in the hop gardens. Her fingers worked fast to tie the blue strands around coconut fibre strings, holding them in place to run four square, dirt to pole top, where they came together as a slender four-sided pyramid reaching high into the air. Under sun and gentle rains throughout the coming summer weeks the hops would race up the strands, reaching for the sky dense with heavy green buds, their overlapping petals forming tightly bound and armoured flowers, their stems winding tough, grasping and fibrous.

Jodi told the rest of the crew and old Nettlesby, whose hops she was twiddling, that she was a traveller. This was true up to a point, but she knew it was really just a summer fiction, one that was seeming less real with each passing year. She stayed on the farm a little longer every summer, often into hop picking, and never managed to go much further. 'Next year,' she would say, before ambling off under lowering autumn skies to find a bus that would take her back to Brighton.

She carried a mandolin and a backpack with the tent for one and sleeping bag, plus her few clothes, pencils, charcoal and sketchbooks. Tall and muscular of build, her oval face has a sharply pointed chin and wide-set eyes. Her eyes are heavily lashed and her dark brown eyebrows contrast with the ash-blonde curls bouncing around her face, despite the strip of scarf twisted around her head to hold them back. Jodi has piercings along the whole of one ear and just a single sapphire stud on the lobe of the other. Her hands have no tattoos but are grubby with 6B graphite and black charcoal dust. It lines her cuticles and stays almost permanently under her nails. She shades and shuffles shadows with her pencils and charcoals, capturing whatever strikes her fancy in soft grey tones.

She peered tentatively out at Sheila from under her straying curls and smiled. A short hug, a cup of tea, a quick look at the bubbling marmalade and the two were soon busy decanting it into the numerous sterile jars parading across Sheila's kitchen table. 'Your timing's pretty good you know, dear. I was wanting to get into the hops meself this spring, but was wondering how, you know, how to go about it.'

Puzzled, Jodi said, 'What do you mean? You're always in the hops this time of year.'

'This year's different. Got a real live one up at the Hall these days. Bonkers he is, you know, worse 'n those Mainwarings and their fireworks, worse 'n that hoity-toity drunken pair, them what nearly drowned in the lake when they tried skinny dippin'. Needs me there every day of the week, he says, eight to ten, and I have to keep out of his sight. Leaves a terrible mess in the kitchen, sleeps in a different bedroom every night. Dirty black clothes always on the floor and old tins of tuna fish and wine bottles all over the place. You never know where you'll find them. You know. He hates the sound of the wash an' the hoover an' plays horrible loud music all the time. Spends his time sitting at his desk in the sun room, you know, even in the rain when he can't see out. But he pays bloody well, so that's why I thought you could do it.'

Confused, Jodi listened to her old friend and waited for a break in the stream of words, watching as Sheila expertly tied string around discs of wax paper neatly centred on the tops of one jar of marmalade after the other. There was something mesmerising in the speed and dexterity in her old hands, which were following a pattern etched over the years into muscle and bone.

'Why don't you just tell him you'll come later? Can you do that, just do a half-day twiddling? Why would I want to do it?' It wasn't a conversation that could go anywhere in its present form and Jodi couldn't quite see what the problem was, why they were having it. Surely this strange man could be flexible?

'I just don't think it's worth the chat, that's all, you know, trying to explain to him about the hops, why it matters an' that. He's not much of a one for traditions, and normally I would just say, you know, that I'm coming in at a different time, but that I'm still coming in. Or that you'd be coming in, if you fancied it, you know. But I don't know how he'd take it, you know.'

Jodi watched the jars being sealed without pause during this speech and said, 'What about just telling him about the hops, about the crew? You could tell him about having not as much energy as you used to for doing two jobs, and that I could do it. But I'm not sure if I want to, but if it's only for a couple of hours a day. Maybe. You said he pays well?'

The marmalade was all safely poured and sealed, the kettle was on and over a strong cup of tea and home-made fruitcake Jodi found herself agreeing to take on the Shadowhurst Hall cleaning job eight to ten Monday to Friday, £135 a week. 'Are you sure?' she had said, in disbelief at both the pay and that Sheila was happy to forego it. She was, so Jodi would go up of a morning and then join Sheila and the others in the hops when she finished at the Hall. They wouldn't say anything to Martin because Sheila never saw him anyway and as long as the work got done, what did it matter who did it. Sheila would get the shopping in and Jodi could take it up to the Hall. Sorted.

'You can stop here in Nora's room if you like, seeing as how, you know, she's wed and gone away to Hurstwell.'

Jodi smiled and nodded. 'That would be great. Thanks. Do you see much of her these days, now that she's so far away? After all, it's nearly eight miles.'

Sheila didn't get the tease, but instead said matter-of-factly,

'Not now she's got her husband and her own life. We're not needed now, you know, not until grandchildren come along.'

And that was that. Jodi went up the narrow stairs to drop her stuff and soon Sheila could hear the trembling tones of the mandolin floating out of the opened windows and meandering their way back down into her sticky kitchen.

***

In silence Martin and Joshua walked through the garden back to the house. It was now mostly white and was starting to look almost welcoming. At least it was losing its desolate air, its sense of abandonment and loneliness. Joshua noted the naked earth now denuded of weeds and reminded himself to check with Alison about the planting. She'd organised the gardeners, who had wreaked havoc on the unsuspecting weeds and liberally fertilised and rotavated the beds into submission. Now they lay bare and open and waiting for new arrivals, new pages waiting to be written. The landscapers were angling for the planting as well, which Joshua didn't want because their list of plants all looked expensive and high maintenance. He wanted black tulips and delphiniums and hollyhocks, flowers that would be stark against the bungalow's white walls, with roses to perk up the sad statues, and yew hedging to slow the wind as it raced headlong across the lawns to the house. Martin had looked blank throughout the plant conversation, nodding as he searched in vain for some point of reference for Calla lilies and black hellebores. He liked the word and said so. Back in the glittering kitchen they found a bag of shopping with chocolate biscuits, bread, cheese and some croissants and a couple of unripe bananas.

'Sheila,' Martin said as Joshua emptied the bag and started cutting into the new loaf.

'No butter,' he observed.

Martin ignored him and said, 'She thinks it's helpful, but it isn't important to me. The croissants are cold.'

Sheila had indeed dropped off the bag, vaguely thinking that Martin might shift a gear one day and fancy something other than tuna fish and fizzy wine. Joshua was glad she had and that in the cupboard she had thoughtfully provided a large jar of local honey as well as some peanut butter.

By the time Martin emerged coughing from his bath and was dressed in dry clothes, Joshua was getting ready to go back to town. Now in chinos, blazer and loafers, his new coat was roughly dry, brushed and safely stowed. He picked up his bag and noted Martin's muddy blue velvet dropped in a corner of the kitchen along with his jeans and boots. They would stay there until Monday, Joshua knew. He had a sudden thought and calling along the hall to Martin he said, 'There were some boxes up there. Do you want to bring them indoors before I go? There might be something interesting.'

Martin, barely recovered from his exertions, bathed, clean-clothed and calming, should really have said no, said he wasn't interested, said he didn't care, said he wanted to stay indoors now. But he said, 'All right. But no, not now. Next time.' And then to his own and Joshua's surprise. 'No wait. Let's do it now. I'll come too. Let's get all of it and put it in the garage.' He retrieved his coat from the floor, coughed his way carefully back into it and picked up the torch conveniently waiting on the windowsill by the back door. Together they stepped out into the growing darkness, Joshua's new green coat back in service and once again getting rain splattered along with his pristine chinos. Birds were darting sharply home and warning loud and urgent of the coming night, of the danger of the dark.

It took longer than they had expected to get back to the ruin as the day slowly faded and the rain melted away the ground. The soft grey light was twisting and sliding away to another distant dawn. It left a myriad of purple and apricot shades streaked and smudged across the sky. The still bare trees stretched black into the fading light and shade. The light was fast turning cold and hard into black. By the time they got to the top of the slope, Martin and Joshua could barely see anything through the damp, dark air. By the time they reached the broken-down folly, it was almost totally dark. The torch in Martin's hand jumped and danced as he stumbled unsteady and hesitant over the undergrowth. Martin was once again coughing hard, and he leaned against a young tree whose upstretched limbs rattled and quivered with his every breath, showering him with water droplets. And something was calling and they unknowingly were following. It would be enough.

'Let's leave the rest for another time,' Martin wheezed, as he hauled at the steamer trunk. They could barely see the thing and it seemed rooted to the slabs of the broken floor. They each grasped a rusty handle, one on either side of the box, leaning into it for balance and ballast. Suddenly uprooted the trunk left an empty space and unseen in the dirt hundreds of unexpectedly disturbed woodlice rallied in panic, their swivelling legs searching randomly for new shelter and confused in the dark, the darkness sought.

Struggling back down through the slippery mud and brambles, the effort brought on more bouts of severe coughing for Martin. Joshua stepped with care to avoid puddles that might splash muddy water onto his clothes. Beneath the sound of their squelching footsteps they heard the rending sound of velvet. Amidst the slithering and stumbling, Martin's sodden coat was losing its battle with the brambles. Joshua was beginning to lose his temper. Why had he even thought of suggesting this ridiculous second excursion. He had had enough of rural now. He had a couple of broken nails and the filthy black mud and the brambles were threatening to ruin his beautiful new coat, as they had already shredded Martin's. Joshua had lost any sense of intrigue, of interest in the mystery. As he slipped and slithered yet again under the weight of the steamer trunk, Joshua comforted himself with the thought that so far his coat's dense tweed was holding off the brambles and the wet. Martin on the other hand was once more sodden, moving colourless in the dark, the hem of his coat torn and dirty. And he was still coughing unrelentingly.

Eventually, they got the box down to the garage where they could take a closer look at it. Under the outside light's sodium glare the trunk was clearly very old, very rusty and covered in decades of grime, wet, sticky and anonymous. But a wipe of waterlogged velvet sleeve and under the dirt they saw RML stamped in faded and fractured white letters. They stayed staring so still for so long that the motion-triggered lights went out and they were left in darkness. Owls called a warning across the sky, tree to tree, wing to wing. A growl and a cough. 'How about you don't go back to town yet? How about we go up to the pub for something to eat? We haven't done that yet. I'll drive there and you can drive back. Then you can get a cab back up to town, if you like. Or from the pub. I can drive back here on my own. I know the way.'

Joshua stared disbelieving and stuttered uncertainly, 'Sounds good to me', his heart pounding, his blush rising, his mood improving. A secret in the darkness. They shoved the trunk to one side and both seriously grubby and wet climbed into the car's immaculate seats, mud and wet streaking its perfect leather with ugly organic graffiti. Snarling its way down the drive, the car's bright lights startled windblown leaves and raindrops danced with the flap and slap of the windscreen wipers. The wind was picking up and it blew leaves and spiteful sticks across their path. The green-eyed stare of deer sheltering under

Shadowhurst's line of dense cedar trees blinked and flickered through the darkness.

They sat in silence as the Ferrari's pistons chanted their hypnotic mantra. The car skidded slightly before finding its grip as it rounded the corner onto the lane and its windows started to blur under its passengers' gently rising steam. Fumbling for the demister Martin inadvertently turned off the wipers, the heater, the lights and the muted radio, progressing in darkness slowly through the watery night and aware that it wasn't really so dark after all.

Joshua's frantic flailing smashed to pieces the minuscule moment in the dark. 'For God's sake, what are you doing... stop... you can't see where you're going', and with the lights on and the windscreen wipers smacking once more, the radio suddenly blared out the final bars of 'West End Blues' and the silent moment was suddenly gone.

'1928. Louis Armstrong and his orchestra,' said Martin hitting the mute button before the radio could make any reply.

Standing by the bar with their filthy clothes and untidy hair, the pair were not entirely out of place in the Swan, the least salubrious of Catsdown's four pubs. Its clientele are still mostly farmers and farm workers, mostly a bit tattered and worn, mostly not fussed about the odd bit of hay or random weeds tagging on for the ride.

'Two pints of Harvey's, please, and can we get some food?'

The barmaid, tall, blonde, heading for forty and a thickening middle, was excessively made up. She knew who they were and noted their wet hair and general dirtiness in a moment before handing them a menu. 'Specials are on the board,' she indicated with a glance as she pulled the second pint before setting the glasses on the bar and taking Martin's credit card.

'We'll be sitting over there,' Joshua said, gesturing to a spot in the corner by the open fire. A table, two seats, a bank of gently flaming logs. Perfect. He ordered food. Martin was coughing profusely and enjoying the wisps of smoke threading their way around the chimney. They sat staring at the fire and the beers, both lost in thought. Martin, despite himself, found that he wanted to know who RML was and Joshua, as always, wanted to know who Martin was.

'You must be the kiddy up at Shadowhurst.' The sudden voice, burred and rasping, cut through their ponderings like a foghorn. Martin stared at the stranger through the flop of damp hair hiding his eyes and said nothing, but shifted his glance to the floor, a hand holding safe his beer. Joshua sank back into his seat and, staring at the fire, was uninterested in conversation with strangers, especially one so shabby and forthright.

'I'm the bloke what's got you your sheep,' the old man persisted, slightly louder and strident through broken teeth and ample spit accumulating in the corners of his mouth. 'I'm your neighbour.' He laughed short and sharp, taking a lubricating swig from his almost empty tankard.

'Nettlesby?' Joshua, unexpectedly shocked that this rumpled old man was not a stranger but an as yet unmet business acquaintance, blushed.

He looked up from the fire as Nettlesby continued, 'The very same. You must be Martin, is it?' He met Joshua's gaze, taking note of Joshua's posh clothes and ignoring his strange-looking friend still staring at the floor.

Martin was counting peanuts someone had dropped and without looking up said, 'I'm Martin. Who are you?'

'Like I said, I'm the bloke what got you your sheep, your neighbour.' Nettlesby broke into a wheezy, cracked laugh.

Coughing in his turn and soaking in the heat, confused and his head starting to buzz, Martin pushed back his hair. He looked at Joshua for explanation, who stared back and raised an eyebrow. Martin slurped at his pint, waiting, and counted the bricks in the inglenook behind them.

'So pint, then?' Nettlesby said as he pulled up a chair to join them at their sticky table for two.

He looked from one to the other, wondering when one of them would say something useful. He laughed again and shook his head. 'Maybe you aren't the talkative types, sheep or no sheep, eh?'

Joshua, suddenly aware of his derelict manners, blurted, 'Of course, Mr Nettlesby, I am so sorry, I wasn't expecting to see you, to meet you... here, or, oh... I'm sorry, yes, please do let me get you a drink. Harvey's, is it?' He stood up, embarrassment rising red and awkward to his cheeks. He waved an introduction to Martin and put out his hand. 'Joshua Fothergill it is. We have indeed spoken at length, and this is Martin.' This last with another wave. Joshua noted that this man had his own slightly battered tankard as he said all this and moving towards the bar, he left Martin alone with his new friend.

'Nettlesby, you said?' Martin ventured, staring at a deeply lined face, dirt ingrained in haphazard creases and thick, bushy grey eyebrows reaching out and upwards. They chased in vain a receding hairline. It marked the shrinking boundary of a shock of short upstanding white hair. Deep in their sockets the eyes were dark and sharp and ageless, and they did not match the face they sat in.

'That's it, boy. You've got some of our sheep for the summer. Something about improving the view your friend said.'

And then Martin was stuck for what to say next. Martin was aware of the sheep and the improved view but had no idea how the sheep got there. They just were. 'What else do you do?' he said, surprising himself that he was genuinely interested.

'Well, we do a bit of it all really. Cattle sometimes, bit of corn, but mostly hops.'

None of this meant anything to Martin but he nodded as sagely as he could. He was starting to catalogue eyebrow hairs as Joshua set down the pints.

Having missed this last bit of chat, he said again, 'We've spoken on the phone, Mr Nettlesby. I'm the one representing Martin and Shadowhurst. Joshua Fothergill. You've got the hops as well, I think.'

Nettlesby's face spread into a chaos of wrinkles and happiness and he added, 'You're drinking them right here and now, 'tis Nettlesby Kent Goldings what goes into Harvey's Best.'

Pondering this curious bit of trivia and wondering what a golding was, Martin sipped at his beer, watching in amazement as Nettlesby 'call me John' gulped down his pint almost in one go before standing and stretching out a welcoming hand.

'Well, that's me, thanks to you both. We'll see you again sometime, I'm sure.' He shook first Joshua's extended hand and waited momentarily for Martin before shaking his too. New friend John put his tankard on the bar, nodded to the room, turned for the door and was gone. Joshua was remembering how much that mandatory post and rail and sheep netting for the top field had cost and wondering if Nettlesby might also be in the fencing line. Martin was wondering when John Nettlesby was born.

Plates of home-made steak and kidney pie and scampi and chips were jockeying for position with the pints and sauces on the too-small table. Martin was too preoccupied to talk as he meticulously separated steak from kidneys and matched the pieces to a specific and unvarying number of peas. The calculation for how many pieces lurking under the pastry would be needed to match even quantities of peas was made as soon as his plate was in front of him. Through random mouthfuls of scampi, squashed peas and chips bound to a mush with tartar sauce, Joshua was on his Blackberry calling for a cab to take him back to Hampstead. Around them the pub was filling up and the sports channel on the widescreen television getting louder, locked in combat with the rising volume of the drinkers shouting at the game, jostling and pushing, laughing and secure on a Saturday night in alcohol's generous and sympathetic arms.

'My cab'll be here in half an hour,' Joshua said, a hint of something wistful in his tone. He went to the bar, and the barmaid, smiling slightly, handed him the bill.

'Shall I put it on the card?' she said, and with a hint of hesitation added, 'so you've met old John, then', fishing for more. She wanted to know something other than their names and address, more details to put together a local picture of these newcomers who never talked to anyone. She wanted them to talk to her, and as she handed over the receipts she wondered why they were both so dirty. It was not what she would have expected and this slightly annoyed her.

***

By the time they left the Swan the rain had stopped. Standing in the car park under a sharp-angled and cloudless night sky, Joshua ventured, 'You know, I could stay until tomorrow, help you go through that trunk, if there's anything in there worth seeing maybe?' He looked at Martin staring up at the night sky, white stars on black, and then added, 'But perhaps it's best not. I've things to do up in town.' Joshua's Sundays were usually spent running in Regent's Park or playing squash. He would usually read the *Economist* cover to cover over a bottle of something delicious and food ordered in. He would doze in the bath over a brandy and put together a clothing plan for the coming week.

Martin was looking at the raindrop patterns on his shiny red and now mud-splattered car. He couldn't think of why he would need help. Out of nowhere came a memory and Martin said, 'We know what we are, but know not what we may be.'

'What? What's *Hamlet* got to do with it?' Joshua replied, confused and sad and awash with the desire that there should be more. More to go back to Hampstead for than tomorrow's squash tournament. More than his weekly conversation with his mother. More than he could have here in this black and diamond-bright night.

'Act 4, Scene 5,' said Martin, 'the bit where she goes mad. Not sure why that matters. Sorry. No. Don't stay. I need some quiet. I'll see you in the week. I'll be at the flat on Wednesday.'

Joshua had expected most of it but not the sorry. Sorry? Since when is Martin ever sorry for anything? The taxi arrived but before Joshua had climbed inside, he was aware of the red Ferrari whisking off through the puddles and out of the car park onto the road, where the car's lights too slowly came on and beamed ahead into the night.

Lurching into his excessively lit garage Martin saw the steamer trunk waiting like a promise to be fulfilled. He sat in the car until the bright lights went off and stared at the faded outlines of the box. It had been safely stowed up there in the woods for how long, he wondered. It looked as if it was aware that it was now out of place and it had an air of teasing, slightly anxious anticipation about it. Maybe Simon or Sheila knew something about the ruin and the boxes, the story of how they got there, whose they were. Maybe there was a clue in those empty bottles. Maybe there was a clue in the box itself. Martin shivered and swung out of the car into the sudden harsh, bright light and made a mental note to get Simon to switch those annoying sensor things off. Alison in overdrive.

Sunday mornings at Shadowhurst were a difficult time for Martin, because no one leaves coffee on the Aga or almond croissants in the Aga's warming oven. No one comes to make his bed or tidy up after him at the weekends, so there are three beds for Sheila to make on Monday mornings. He cannot sleep in an unmade bed at Shadowhurst. He has to shut the door on each rumpled bedroom he sleeps in. He is afraid to see the mess. Along with the risk of breaking the self-imposed smoking ban, weekends pose a very real risk that Martin might start to turn his country refuge into a different version of his London squalor. This he does not want. When he is alone, he spends Saturdays at his desk drawing straight-lined versions of the trees twisting in the distance or he walks along the lake stalking the swans and trying not to cough. On Sundays, weary with the resistance effort, he drinks and listens to music all day long. He drinks a lot, starting in the morning in the bath, which he leaves unemptied for Sheila to deal with the next day. The music is courtesy of a stack of CD players hidden in a cupboard and playing many hours' worth of random tunes on shuffle, sometimes matching Martin's mood and increasingly not. That particular Sunday was no different, despite the box waiting for Martin in the garage. He drinks more and, singing, ambles for countless hours around his courtyard, now emptied of the remnants of someone else's life. Eventually, he fades away completely.

***

Monday morning found him still dressed and asleep in the corridor near the kitchen. He woke up to the music continuing to pound on its endless shuffle and aware of a colossal headache that seemed to be keeping the beat. He staggered to the sitting room and reaching to the back of the CD players' cupboard pulled the power plug with immense energy and satisfaction. The morning quiet washed over him and as the new spring light strengthened he fell back to sleep again on the sofa, remembering the trunk as he slid into a semi-sleep, cursing the noisy birds and the brightness of the light seeping its sly way behind his eyelids. He gave up and figured that by now Sheila would have done his coffee and almond croissant and be busying herself emptying baths and making beds, out of his sight.

But in the kitchen were hot coffee and pastries nowhere to be seen. A quick look at the clock and its dancing numbers, bouncing painfully to the rhythm of his heart, and Martin realised he was still on his own. It was too early. The stuff in the bag from Saturday was gone except for one sad and crumbling croissant, and there was no choice but to try to make his own coffee. There was no trendy coffee place to call and get it delivered at a staggering premium. But how hard could it be? He found the coffee grinder, a cup, and beginning to feel a slight tingle of victory put the kettle on. A nasty dry hissing noise and a click told Martin that the battle was barely begun. He had to try again, and this time with water. He stared with intense malevolence at the kettle, now satisfied and starting at first with a slow murmur gradually growing towards exuberant release. Now for the coffee, he thought to himself with just a hint of smug; he could do the grinding while the kettle was doing its thing. He might even put that tired old croissant in the oven, he pondered, feeling strangely pleased with himself. It was short-lived.

Jodi stood in the back doorway and watched as Martin fought frantically to get the lid off the coffee tin. As coffee beans exploded around the kitchen and he struggled to catch them as they flew, Jodi started to smile.

As he reached down to the floor and slipped on a few stray beans, he shouted out 'Bloody 726 of you buggers everywhere and all I need is fifty-two.' He heard her polite cough and turned on his bottom to look up. 'It's not funny. Who are you and what do you want?' From his position on the floor Martin could see a very tall, very tanned woman, slender and fair-haired with the same blue eyes as him, except that Jodi's eyes were warm and laughing.

'Sheila sent me,' she said. 'We're in the hop gardens together, but she said you paid better, and Sheila wants a couple of days twiddling in the open air.'

Hammers and cymbals were now crashing arrhythmically behind his eyes. Martin could only scowl. She spoke but she made no sense. Twiddling in the open air? 'What?' he said as Jodi found a dustpan and brush and cleared up the beans.

'Have some water while I do the coffee.' She handed him a glass, peering down at him stern-faced and serious. 'If you want me to go I can, but Sheila didn't think you'd notice, as long as the job got done. You weren't supposed to be up yet. It's only half seven.'

All this information was far too much for Martin's bruised brain to take. He looked up at her and then turned onto his knees to stand. The reflex movement into his pocket prompted Jodi to say, 'It's okay. Sheila told me the rules. I'll go away and come back again, shall I? Shall I do the coffee first? And I've got the almond croissants here for you.' Hesitating she put the bag on the Aga and then, bolder, started grinding coffee. 'I won't take a minute.'

Martin, by now upright, peered at her for a few seconds from behind his hair before heading off to find a bed that was freshly made. When he had woken up a couple of hours later and had showered and dressed, he was alone and all the other beds were made and all the bathrooms immaculate. On the Aga in the kitchen were still warm coffee and pastries.

He spent the rest of the day in his glass room drawing black-and-white line illustrations of the woods where he and Joshua had found the ruin and the boxes. The trees Joshua had arranged to get cut down and turned into logs were neatly stacked, curing ready for next winter, and the view was more expansive, open, a new landscape. Now that he was drawing the shapes of the walls, he could see the structure's outlines and more hiding in the greening trees and brambles and curiously in his imagination. Those arches he realised were part of an old wine store, hence the empty bottles. Once they were gone whoever used to go up to the folly must've stopped going there, probably when the wine ran out. He could see the water trickling down to the lake, along a brown crack in the green, and he could see the curling ripples of the water as it touched the lake's placid, silent surface. His day was now calm and lined, directed and steady, and unexpectedly the shock of someone new in his life was soon absorbed.

Besides his unexpected conversation with Jodi, that day he spoke only to Simon. Simon wanted to collect some new chains he'd ordered for his chainsaw, so he would be late bringing in wood for the fire. Why that mattered Martin wasn't sure but as he was leaving to run his errand Martin called him back. 'What do you know about that old shack up in the woods?'

'Shack?' Simon answered, running his hand across his head and miraculously not upsetting the quiff. 'There's no shack up there. You must mean the old folly, what got turned into a place for the old lady.'

'What old lady? Who are you talking about?'

Simon frowned, his hand still on his head, and considered awhile. 'Well, the old lady what lived at the old 'all before it got tore down. She offered it up for a nospital in the war and it got wrecked. After the war there was no money to repair it, so she sold it for demolition like, except then she 'ad nowhere to go. They gave her an old caravan to live in and fixed up the folly so that she'd have somewhere for all 'er bits and pieces, them as wouldn't fit in the caravan.' He paused a moment. 'You don't want to be bothering with that old place. It got knocked to bits in the hurricane in 1987. Leave it to the weeds. I'll be off now, then?' His query was unanswered as Martin stood staring. Simon hovered in his socks wanting to get on and get his chains before the ironmonger's closed.

'Right,' Martin said. 'It's a mess up there. We walked up on Saturday.' The memory brought on a bout of coughing that Simon took as his cue to leave. Through his cough Martin shouted out, 'And switch those bloody light sensors off before you go.'

Lists

It was evening before Martin ventured out to the garage to investigate the trunk. He stood there in the near dark and stared at it, his bottom lip sucked in under his teeth, his brain teeming with speculations. Suspicious of its weight he wanted to open it, and yet perhaps it was too soon. Perhaps it would be better in daylight or with someone else there to share this secret, this puzzle that he might not be able to unpick. Or perhaps it was only heavy because it was full of mud and dirt, and there was nothing interesting in it, to share or otherwise. In the night beyond he heard the owls again and found himself humming 'Black Cat Hoot Owl Blues', remembering Ma Rainey singing 'it's bad luck if I stay here, it's still more bad luck if I die', and the thought of death and dying suddenly overwhelmed him and the Pol Roger beckoned him back indoors.

But the Pol Roger siren's voice faded as Martin crunched across the gravel back to the house. Instead he made a cup of instant coffee, scattering 203 little brown granules across the countertop, leaving it as a teasing greeting for Jodi in the morning. Standing in front of the open fridge, Martin used the ring-pull lid from a tin of tuna fish as a spoon. After polishing off his supper, he took his coffee, and unaware that he was slop-

ping its upper millimetres into the scattered message, sloped off
down the hall to his glass room. He wanted to work some more
on his drawings of swans, carefully and precisely crafted from
overdrawn lines and curves of varying widths, black on white
turning white on black. Outside a different blackness wrapped
itself around the bright shining room and held it fast in the
night. Martin stared back and forth, out to the black and back
to the brightly lit room, his measured black lines blossoming
out across the naked white of the page. The swans were slowly
turning and turning from black to white under his hand. Lines
and curves drawn over and over until the black outlines of
Martin's swans were become the shadows behind them, and
they mere bleached silhouettes in an inky night.

***

Early the next morning Martin was pressed and dressed and
waiting when Jodi came into the kitchen. She started visibly as
she opened the door and saw her strange boss sitting with one
leg bent across the other, foot jiggling. His hands were behind
his head, which was thrown back to keep his hair out of his
eyes as he watched the back door for her to come. He wasn't
exactly smiling, but he was clearly and exactly waiting.

'Good morning,' she said with a slight hesitance, her head
to one side and an eyebrow raised. She smiled slightly and put
the bag of shopping on the table in front of him, before taking a cloth and wiping away the coffee debris in a single swipe.
'Is there something special you want done?' she ventured, confused to see him after all she had been told.

Martin was coughing and clearing his throat through her
little greeting so he didn't catch a word. 'Can you help me
carry something in from the garage? I need it,' he spluttered.
Relieved that there was nothing amiss, just an early start and
an apparent lack of concern that she was visible to him, Jodi
returned to the back door, opened it with a purposeful flourish

and said 'lead on'. She stood aside and followed Martin as he marched out, coat swirling and moving with unexpected and uncharacteristic speed.

When they got to the garage Simon was already doing something important to a very large sit-on mower. 'Ready for the first cut of the year,' he said with satisfaction as the engine spluttered and coughed into life, writing ciphers in wispy serifs across the new day. 'Sounds a bit like you, Martin,' Simon shouted over the noise, expecting to be told to switch off the racket. But Martin peered through the smoke and said, 'Help us with this first.'

Simon looked with some consternation at the trunk and its white-letter insignia and switched off his mower. 'Where'd you get that, then?' he asked and Martin, sucking in the remnants of petrol fumes still hanging in the air, replied, 'Up at that folly thing, the place I asked you about.'

Simon took a closer look. 'I remember those initials, but I can't rightly remember why.' His voice trailed away and he spat on his hands. He reached for one of the side handles, expecting Martin to reach for the other but Jodi got there first.

With Simon on one side and Jodi on the other, the trunk, dropping dirt and rust dust along the way, was lugged into the house and placed next to Martin's desk. He remembered to say thank you to them both and 'get me something to open this, would you' to Simon. Then he remembered to tell Simon not to mow until tomorrow, when Martin would be up in town and away from the noise. Simon and Jodi went back to the kitchen and sat having coffee, wondering what was so special about the trunk to get Martin up so early.

The trunk was not as small as it had seemed up in the woods, and on closer inspection Martin saw that it was bound with two reinforcing straps of wood and that it had three locks. The big one in the middle was flanked by two smaller ones, and all three had corroded into solid gritty rust, drying since the sojourn in the garage and now leaving faint amber dust flakes on Martin's immaculate beech floor. By the time Simon returned with an array of tools and a cup of coffee for him, Martin found his heart unaccountably beginning to beat just a little bit faster and the pulse in his head starting to rise. Taking his coffee with a shaky hand he said, 'What do you think is in it? It's pretty heavy.'

As Martin slurped and shivered, suddenly chilled, Simon pursed his lips. Then blowing through pursed lips he pondered the question, mindful of his mower waiting and getting wet in the rain that was starting to fall. 'Well,' he said, 'could be anything really. She was a funny old bird. Kept to hersel', never sin 'er much in the village, just to get 'er shopping like. Never really moved on from the war really, never got over 'ow everything changed when 'er daughter left her all alone and she couldn't keep the 'all on 'er own.' Martin looked out from his hair, sapphire-hard blue eyes pressing Simon on. He continued: 'Well, she lost 'er 'usband to the pneumonia like and then when the daughter went off to Canada, well, the ol' lady 'adn't anythin' to much bother with.'

'What happened to her?' Martin said.

'Well, she died a course, like we all do. Went into hospital with a chesty cough and niver came out. They cleared out the caravan. Probably forgot about that place up there.' And with that he nodded slowly, waiting in case there was something more. When there wasn't, either in his memory or Martin's curiosity, he took the empty coffee cup from Martin's hand. Careful not to slip in his socks on the polished floor he headed slowly in the direction of his boots and the mower, to rescue it from the rain and ready it anew for tomorrow's excursion.

Martin waited until he heard the back door close and could see Simon at the mower before dropping to the floor to check

out the tools, sending the russet dust floating yet further afield.
The tool bag contained some long screwdrivers and a couple
of hammers, plus a crowbar, which seemed to Martin excessive
but which reminded him of his dad. His dad kept a crowbar
on the floor of the cab, next to his driver's seat, just in case.
There were twenty-seven different items in the tool bag, most
of which were familiar from the house in Glenkiln Drive and
some of which were completely alien to Martin. He spent a little while picking up each tool, weighing it in his hands and
placing it into one of two groups. Eventually, he had a suitable selection which he then lined up in a neat row, smallest to
largest, and each precisely five millimetres apart from its neighbours, and returned the rejects to the tool bag. He took a deep
breath and sat at his desk looking out at the drizzle as the sun's
light stretched down to turn each droplet into its own magic
prism. The coffee had warmed him and the buzz in Martin's
head was easing. Through rain-washed rainbow light he could
see the greening trees and the fields turning slowly from their
winter torpor. Under the rain and the warmth awakening, he
was ready to tackle the box.

In fact, the box put up no fight at all, which was a bit of a let-
down after all Martin's anticipation of a complicated struggle.
The frozen joints of its dead reddened hinges had eased in the
dry and shelter of the garage. The dirt fastening the trunk tight
had dried and loosened and much of its seal had fallen away
with the movement of being carried, first to the garage and
then, slightly drier, to the house. The central lock had yielded
to Martin's first prise with the largest screwdriver, and the two
on the sides to solid whacks with the mallet. The ferrous dust
danced across the floor, released to tell its own story, tracing
curious shapes and patterns in clusters and lines across the soft
beech wood grain. Martin lifted the lid, which crackled and
softly squeaked, letting loose another fall of dirt and rust, with a

little pitter-pattering sound. He could hear his heart pounding louder and louder in his chest. Breathing slowly and audibly, suppressing a shattering cough, he saw that the trunk was lined in what was once a pale pink taffeta. Now it was spotted and stained in ugly browns and greys, but this box was clearly once a luxury edition. Inside was a jumble of papers, small boxes, folders, books and oddly a pair of women's shoes, twisted and dried with time, the stitching around their peephole toes loosened and colourless. The whole was gritty with decay and dead insects and dirt; the scent of long-dead mould stretched out into the air, rising up and reaching around Martin's shoulders, teasing his senses.

One by one Martin removed each article from the trunk, returning to his desk item by item to record the growing inventory. He carefully dusted off each letter and book, each brochure and picture, measuring them all and counting pages without looking at the contents. The forgotten shoes he left until last. He placed each piece on the floor in a tidy row in the hallway out of the light. He listed everything in careful detail on a fresh white A3 sheet in his perfect Rotring hand. 'Steamer Trunk Contents', the date and time goose-stepped across the sheet's top edge. The list of items, their dimensions, special characteristics and a short description for each, soon grew to fill the whole page.

The trunk held a miscellany of forty-three personal effects, mostly papers, books and letters, some of them unfinished. There was a birthday card written by a grown-up with children's signatures, a train schedule for London to Southampton trains, and one from Catsdown to town. A brochure for the *Mauretania* promised five or six days of fine food and other delights on board the luxury liner in block bold type with a fabled version of New York City in the background. 'Getting there is half the fun', it promised, and in its pages were pictures of cabins and staterooms, the Grand Hall, all vaulted ceilings and plush furniture and wood panelling and drifting chandeliers. Also in the box there were faded rosettes for gymkhanas and agricultural shows, 1941 Best in Show, 1942 Reserve Champion. And a miscellany of photographs, disordered, muddled and jumbled in amongst the trunk's other contents.

One of the photos captured Martin momentarily, and just long enough for the face to stick to the back of his eyes while he was writing down in tidy letters: 15.24 x 10.16 cm black-and-white-and-brown picture of a soldier in uniform. Martin looked at it more carefully and saw that he was standing on a short flight of stone steps in front of a balustrade, near some stone lions. Martin tried to picture the young man just before and just after the photograph was taken, but he couldn't. Turning it over, Martin read 'To my darling Ruth' and saw that it was signed with a flourish 'Charles, December 1944'. As he put it down on his desk the wind outside, now blustery, threw a tangle of rain at the glass and Martin put down his pen. His list was long, and he had not really examined any of the items, but it was getting late. Martin smiled at the box and then smiled again as Billie Holiday sang out 'Isn't this a lovely day, to get caught in the rain'. He could wait and have another lovely day caught in the rain like this.

Lying on the sofa listening to Glenn Miller, Martin was staring at the picture of Charles. He was in uniform, so he was a soldier, and Charles was very fond of his darling Ruth. And then what? Was she his sister or his auntie or his lover, or just a friend? Maybe everyone was darling then, back in 1944? Something about apple trees penetrated his conscience and Martin paid attention as the Andrews sisters told him 'don't sit under the apple tree'. He stared at the ceiling and drifted slowly into Roger's, or was it Pol's, welcoming arms, confused that he could not clearly see the world Ruth and Charles inhabited and wondering how he could find out more, about Pol and Roger, and about Ruth and Charles, and dozed off to sleep.

***

The next morning Martin's first thought was that the letters were a clue and the diaries, scraps of entries in a woman's hand. On the first page the 1945 diary said 'Ruth Margaret Lorne 1945' and underneath it, in block capitals, 'OUR YEAR'. But there was little in the day-to-day entries to tell Martin much about Charles. He learned about hospital discharges and changes on the ward and how the kitchens were doing their best with what they could get from the garden and scant rations. The harvest in 1944 had been good apparently but there was worry about insects and the lack of muck being spread. He learned of dances in the village hall and of the Canadian Spitfire pilots shot down over Normandy still recuperating in the library and how much they enjoyed Wednesday evening singalongs, and Glenn Miller in particular. He read of Ruth's dutiful concern for her parents and the strain this makeshift hospital was putting on them. They really were too old to cope with all the change, all the chaos in the house, the noise, the wounds and operations, the stretched rations and the bitter cold. He read of 'difficulties with Mummy again' but could find no details. He read of a lovely golden locket Charles had given her for her birthday.

Martin found himself puzzling more and more about who this young woman was, and who Charles was. He needed facts. He needed information before he could get a picture beyond this binary black-and-white outline. He wanted a picture. Sitting at his desk that morning, lines all of equal length stepped slowly across his page, marching in a steady squadron, in perfect time. He turned them left and right, in perfect unison, to form an empty rectangle framed in tightly regimented and incrementally angled lines. He stared and stared at the blank space in its centre. To no one he said, 'I'll catch the train back to town. I need to talk to Alison. I need to talk to Roger.' And then he took a clean sheet of paper and started his pen to marching once again, but this time with shorter lines drawn closer together in clipped and perfect lock-step. But he didn't catch the train. He waited until lunchtime and then drove alone and slowly back to his London flat. He left the car parked outside his building and waved to the approaching traffic warden, who was getting to know Martin's car quite well.

A couple of weeks later, following his short but unsatisfying sojourn in town, Martin was back at Shadowhurst. He was waiting for Roger for information, for data. After their initial conversation, Roger had told him he would be in touch, but it had been days and days since they had talked about Shadowhurst and its history. Lines and lines marched black, precise and orderly, and Martin waited until they reached the edge of the page. Then, his knee jiggling and his hair much pulled, Martin waited until he heard the hoover running and slipped out through the kitchen to find Simon.

Not being one to rush into much of anything, Simon was struggling to attach a small trailer to an ancient tractor. 'Off to pick up some more of that wood I am, Martin,' he said by way of a greeting. Adding, 'They've done a fair job of clearing them trees, and all that wood'll see us through for a fair few years.' Up early again, are we, he was pondering, wondering whether this was a good sign or the first signs of another flight.

'I need you to take me to the station as soon as you can. When do the trains go?' Martin was wheezing and standing very close to Simon as he said this, his hand holding back his hair and his eyes laser sharp darting from side to side as he struggled to control the rattling with a series of dry little coughs. Impatient and twitching at his hair, he waited for the endlessly slow response.

'Well, I'm not really sure, Martin, that's the truth of it. But we can find out and Jodi's the one to ask.' Together they turned for the house where they could see Jodi through a window shaking a duvet back into place. "Ere, Jodi, you know about trains, don't you?' Simon bellowed while Martin hovered, fidgeting and anxiously clearing his phlegmy throat.

Jodi stuck her head out of the window, assessing the question because of course Simon knew she would have no idea at all about trains. It was just a ploy to get her to look up train times instead of doing it himself. Jodi considered calling him on it and figured it wasn't worth the bother and would be mean besides. 'Oh, yes, me, of course, all about them,' she said as she retreated back indoors to plump up heavy goose down pillows. But she soon had her phone out and was already tip tap tapping away. 'Where from and what time?'

'From here and as soon as possible,' Martin hissed, scowling as he paced in short strides on the gravel. 'Simon's driving me to the station and getting me a ticket.' Martin's hands started to shake as he made this declaration and the reality of what he was proposing started to sink in. Where was Joshua, he needed Joshua to help him.

Jodi interrupted. '10:23, which is in about half an hour. You've masses of time.' And she shut the window to end the conversation and went back to the last of her cleaning.

'Well, do you want to go now, Martin, and wait at the station, or shall we sit a while and then go?' Simon, leaning lazy and languorous against the recently painted wall, watched as Martin pressed at his phone, increasingly anguished and still pacing. It was going to be a long morning, Simon pondered, ambling over to the car and steeling his resolve to get it out of the garage without mishap. As it roared awake, Simon felt again that rush of passion and heat as he shoved down on the clutch and put the car sharply into gear. Reversing very slowly he thought to himself, that's a new one. Gently, gently, girl, gently, gently, easing off the accelerator more than he felt he should in anticipation of that sudden leap, only this time backwards. But his newly tender touch meant that the red siren complied and moved backwards as cautiously as requested, without the slightest hint of a leap. He drew parallel with Martin as he paced, took her out of gear and gave the pedal just a little push. He smiled a secret smile at the purring response, a response just for him, his own, a secret gift from the voluptuary to him.

Martin cut across their intimate moment though, saying, 'Thanks, Simon. I'll do the driving there and you can bring the car back. I'll call you when I need to be picked up.' Martin clambered into the swiftly vacated driver's seat and immediately gunned it, loud and long that angry roar, before settling her down to a soft murmur and heading very, very slowly down the drive. But when he reached the lane his nerve gave out so he stopped the car. 'You drive. I don't know where the station is.' And standing on the lane waiting for Simon to get out and take his place, Martin noticed that his fences were no longing dragged under and drowning beneath dead weeds. He saw that he had post and rail fencing with sheep netting the whole length of his drive and along the lane. He stared as they drove past it and looked back at his white house with a strangely alien sense of distance. 'How far is it and what time is it?'

Simon looked at the clock on the dash. 'You've got twenty minutes before the train and it takes nine to get to the station.'

'Then slow down, would you. I can't stand waiting on the platform, and you need to get me a ticket.' Rummaging in the glovebox he pulled out a tangle of £20 notes and handed them to Simon.

'One way or return?' he said, but Martin was counting fence

posts and working out how many wire squares were in each bay. He said nothing until Simon handed him his tickets and pointed at the platform on the other side of the tracks, with a nod. Simon put the balance of the cash back in the glovebox and confirmed, 'I'll wait for your call later, then?'

'Yes. Later,' said Martin. 'Later.'

A curious encounter

Alison Cox had always had a plan. Thanks to her unerring determination that she should succeed, she had managed to achieve all that her parents had hoped for their little girl. They just wanted her to have a better life than they had had. But Alison had wanted much, much more than this, much more than a narrow little life living in a narrow little house, scrabbling to get by, on a featureless path to death. But she had listened when her parents told her to work hard at school and she had believed it when her teachers told her that she was bright and capable. She had paid particular attention when she heard stories of girls getting pregnant in their teens and having to live at home with their parents, because no one else wanted them and their bastard children. Not that for Alison, not that. She set her sights instead on the worlds she saw on television growing up in the eighties, like those clever people on *Antiques Roadshow* or Audrey in *To the Manor Born*, except without being broke.

Alison knew that for her the quickest route to an identity far away from the fools and horses world she was living in was marriage. She knew that to marry a character from a posh television programme required education. University would be her hunting ground for such a mate. That was her focus from the first time her mother told her to mind her own business, to comfort her baby brother and dry his tears. 'I'm going to have a nanny,' thought Alison, as she hugged her little brother and plotted her escape. She met Roger at Exeter where they were both studying art history. Avuncular, slightly plump and an unenergetic twenty-two, Roger was on track to take over the family auction house. He recognised in Alison's stolid reliability and doggedness a partner that could help him turn his father's creaking enterprise into a powerhouse in the trade. Theirs was a courtship more of practicalities than passion. Each recognised in the other material they could work with. Romance had come into the picture as an afterthought, but slowly and surely it had come. Within a few short years they had courted, married, had two children and together got the business back on track. Lifted from its knees, Gilbert & Partners now stood tall and proud on the London and Home Counties auction scene. In sentimental moments Roger would toast his old man and wipe away the occasional tear. Family life was making him soft, he told himself. Roger and Alison together and exhaustingly were raising their obnoxiously bright and sporty little girls, little girls whose parents adored them more than they ever thought was possible. A brace of cats and some Labradors completed the picture. All that was missing was Pony Club and gymkhanas and local politics. But there was still time for all that.

Alison and Roger were sitting at a large table in their warehouse in Fulham. They were surrounded by dust-sheeted furniture, paintings and storage crates, all labelled and ready for upcoming sales. They were sorting through several piles of old books, a job lot from a country house clearance. When Martin appeared in the doorway, both were visibly shocked, although Roger marginally less so. He hadn't told Alison about the curious conversation he had had with his brother-in-law some weeks earlier.

'What on earth are you doing here?' Alison squeaked, jumping up from the cluttered table and hurrying over to her brother. 'Is everything all right?' She pawed at him and Martin felt himself shrinking, almost pulling away from his purpose as Alison's eyes darted over him like high-velocity artillery fire.

'For God's sake, Alison, leave the man alone, won't you. Pleased to see you, old man,' said Roger, pushing past his fussing wife and reaching out his well-fed hand in a gentle, soft-skinned welcome. Roger has that air of self-assurance, that confident manner of a man supremely untroubled by life, confident that he can fit smoothly into any situation, that he'll always know what to do, what to say. He's a kind man, a man raised with total love and support, educated, focused and self-assured, fearless in his world. He's still portly with a round, generous face, an open smile and shrewd eyes that pierce straight to the point of most discussions. He inhabits a small but comfortable world, lives a small but contented life, a life where he and Alison share the careful unfolding of their life's story secure almost to the point of smug.

'Must say I was surprised to get your call,' he chortled, looking slightly askance at his wife and waiting for the fireworks. Alison did not disappoint.

'What call? What are you talking about? Martin hasn't called us,' she blurted, nervously tucking her hair behind her ears, shoulders hunched and stepping slightly from side to side as if readying herself to take a punch at some invisible opponent. As his brother-in-law gave a surreptitious wink, before raising his eyebrows at Alison and uttering a long and questioning 'hmmmm', Martin's buzzing head started calming. He held on to the plan, kept his mind's eye on the objective, took a deep breath and with his hand in his pocket patted his leg with some urgency.

'What have you found out?' he said, and Alison looked back and forth between the two, confused again and now curious.

'What's going on?' she repeated, folding her arms, resting one foot, hips forward, vaguely noting the absence of a cigarette and that Martin had filled out a little.

With a few brief words her husband explained that Martin was interested in the history of Shadowhurst Hall. He explained that Martin had asked if he could help find out more about it. 'Drama over, dear,' he concluded, with another long 'hmmmm?'

'So what have you found?' Martin repeated, elbow raised, his hair clasped tight at the back of his head, holding on. He took a seat at the overloaded table.

'Well, not a lot,' Roger replied with a sigh as he went to put the kettle on. 'The place was requisitioned in 1916 as a military hospital and again in 1944, but it didn't work out quite so well in the second war as it had in the first. The place was older and more run down of course, fewer staff, less money and all that. It had been used for refugees, evacuated children, as a school. It didn't take to the increased activity in 1944. And of course there were a lot more men coming in from the coast, a lot of pilots. Our boys and Jerries. Some of the men who died there are buried in the village. Mostly the place was trashed, so old Lady Lorne had to sell up. She sold it for scrap to be recycled into new housing. Chap who bought it made a killing of course. She and his Lordship were already past it really. It was the daughter, Ruth, who seems to have been the driver for the hospital, but then she went off to Canada. Eloped. I've found a bill of sale for the house in 1950 and another reference you might find interesting. It seems they had the police interview the whole village when the girl left. Lady Lorne couldn't believe she'd gone off with her captain, but that's what she did. He was Canadian. That's probably where she went.' He handed Martin a box file with the bill of sale for Shadowhurst, various auction catalogues, some old maps and a miscellany of dusty papers. There was a copy of an ancient police report documenting a village meeting, the people attending and their group conclusion that Ruth Margaret Lorne and Captain Charles Hickson of the 406 Squadron Royal Canadian Air Force had run away together, presumably back to where he was from. According to the report several witnesses confirmed that they had seen her leave the house in the very early morning, dressed for travelling and with her suitcase and heading for the woods in the direction of the station. They said she'd had another row with her mother, a not uncommon occurrence apparently. There was a picture of Ruth, dark-haired and smiling, and around her neck a little heart-shaped locket. A letter with details of when and where to meet Charles in London was referenced as part of the evidence. Case closed and a note of thanks to Lord and Lady Lorne for the tea and sandwiches, despite the rationing. A couple of official stamps and a mark in red denoting where the report had been filed. End of story.

'This is great,' Martin said, glancing through the pages. 'Joshua's given me a list of the owners, after the war, but this is much more interesting.'

'Why?' Alison was bent looking over Martin's shoulder as he went through the documents. 'Why is it so interesting?' she repeated.

Martin twisted away from the warmth and damp of her lingering breath and looked up at her and wondered when she would see that he was gone. 'It's the house, the space, I want to know more about it, that's all. I'm really not sure why, what the point is, but I just do.'

Alison glanced at her husband as he handed over a dainty cup of tea, with not a drop spilled in the equally dainty saucer. Was this what they had hoped, something stepping away from the darkness. The three of them sat in silence, drinking tea and eating chocolate biscuits. Roger went back to the books and his inventory, humming softly to himself while Alison waited for Martin to tell her more about the house. But he didn't. Instead, he drained his cup and reached for three dark digestives before picking up the box file and getting up.

He left her sitting there, confusion drifting about her head, almost visible and impenetrable. As he approached the door to leave, Martin turned around and suggested that they both come down to see him some weekend. 'Lots of good walks, and the local pub isn't too bad. You'll like it. Bring the girls.'

Staring at his disappearing back, the bone china cup halfway to her mouth, Alison could only utter, 'Good lord... right... yes, of course.' Roger carried on going through the books in search of elusive first editions and copies that were not too far gone for an auctioned job lot. He sighed and looking over his bifocals was in time to see the swirl of blue velvet caress the warehouse door in a whispered but purposeful goodbye.

For the train back to Catsdown, Martin had to count his way from the cab to the departures board to check his train's platform. He knew that he had four minutes to catch his train because he had told the cab driver the exact time he wanted to arrive at the station and requested a route that would deliver him there to the minute. The driver had risen admirably to the challenge, deviating without appearing to take a longer route, and considered his efforts worthy of performance art. 'An artiste,' he told Martin, 'that's what I am, mate, an artiste.' Martin had commended him and tipped him excessively for his artistry, before calculating the number of steps into the station, the platform number probabilities and how many carriages the train would likely have.

Head down he weaved his way through the people standing staring at the departures board, staring at their phones, staring into space, waiting and watching. To Martin they all looked the same, a forest of shapes and sizes that hadn't varied in years. They were the same people he saw on the 93 bus, the same people in the wine bars, walking in the park or hovering on the pavements waiting to cross the road. He focused on his steps and the train and was relieved that the train had the same number of coaches as the one coming up to town, and that it left from the same platform. He sat breathing deeply, with his hands clasped around the box file Roger had given him. He was aware of a residual and familiar wheeze as his ribcage rose and fell more slowly. He sat on the same side of the train going down as coming up and counted the same number of seats in the carriage, but different numbers of seats occupied versus seats unoccupied. The people were all the same, anonymous.

His calculations, the steady breathing, the edges and corners of the box file with its calming pages full of printed facts felt safe in his hands. Along with the rhythm of the train they kept his mind purring mechanically along for the journey's duration when, after an hour or so, the next challenge was coming. Simon had driven Martin to the station, and Martin was supposed to have called him to arrange getting picked up. Except that Martin hadn't, deliberately ignoring his own plan, wanting instead to walk back to Shadowhurst from the station alone, wanting to see how it would be to be random, no control, no backup. But Martin didn't know the way and didn't have a map, so random brought with it certain terrors. He checked his phone again for charge, for signal, for the reassurance that his random could be cut at any moment with a simple call to Simon.

Stepping off the train at Catsdown Holt, he moved gentle and slow into the lazy hum and tweets of a balmy afternoon, then stood still a moment. He was hearing the birds. The distant train whistles were surfing the soft air, riding the final floating ripples before fading away into distant and unfamiliar vistas. His whistling chest a gentle counterpoint to the unpatterned birdsong, Martin watched the other two disembarking passengers walk to their cars, parked with others in a messy line along the lane. He had a direction and, tailing his fellow passengers, decided that he would just take the road and route that Simon had followed that morning. It was a picture in his head he had only to mirror. And it was random enough. The thought of crossing the fields to where he knew his house was brought to mind images of war zones and desolation, and a terrain untouchable, rising unknown anxieties that brought the hissing back into his head.

He set off marching forwards with his eyes half closed, taking furtive looks around him, anxious that the quiet and the sound of his own footsteps might mask something alien and unknown, some reckonless surprise. The solid box file under his arm reassured him. But nothing to count, no lines and cracks underfoot, nothing for his mind to calculate. Except that Martin could soon calculate as he walked. He counted his footsteps and the number of gates he passed and how many bars and diagonals they had, the numbers of drains, closed and uncovered, round and rectangular, and the numbers of cars overtaking him as he walked along. Numbers. Coming to the top of a small hill he could see in the distance the edge of a flat white building, Shadowhurst. The lakes and woods were hidden in the curve of the hill facing his house, but Martin knew what he was looking at, although not quite what he could really see.

He was growing bolder and slightly too warm so he took off the heavy velvet coat and, feeling oddly brave, took a turn to the left, off the path, to climb over a farm gate (five bars, one diagonal and two uprights) and head in an exact and alien line of unknown adventure towards Shadowhurst, box file in hand and heart beating fast. More than off the map.

The sun was shining and as he stomped along the edge of a newly ploughed field he could count the furrows and the number of shiny black crows stepping lazily along them. They watched him with cautious suspicion as he moved closer. When he got too close they floated up and away on gleaming black wings spread indolent and careless, carbon smudges on the sky's blue perfection. He was coughing hard again with the exertion as he made his way slowly through the heavy ground and up the hill. A curious sense of anticipation was rising as he approached Shadowhurst. Passing down through a messy farmyard he found an encouraging sign identifying this part of his route as a public footpath. He couldn't see the house anymore. It was hidden in a fold of woods and sloping fields, but he was comfortable with its image pasted uppermost in his head, a beacon to bring him home.

Pausing to catch a bigger breath and slow his thudding heart, he watched an aimless hen scratching vigorously at a patch of dusty dirt and as she took a sudden dive at whatever it was she sought, he understood that she had purpose and direction after all. The hen, arrayed in glamorous fawn with copper highlights that glinted bright in the sun, pecked towards him as he stood. She turned a beady eye in his direction, quizzical, assessing, as he coughed again and shifted his weight and the box file to the other hip. Head on one side as the coat softly swayed on his arm, she weighed up the possibility of the movement having

shed an insect or two, decided not and turned away to keep
working her way through the dust. Other hens, some white
with blood-red combs and lurid yellow legs, some a mass of
grey, white, black and brown speckles with feathered feet and
combs hanging jauntily to one side, came gradually into view.
They ambled their lazy ways around him, a random collection of subdued polite strangers moving in a gently murmur-
ing arc. Martin was almost afraid to disturb their deliberations,
but pushing his hair behind his ears, chin up and eyes ahead,
he stepped forward into their sudden swirl and cackle, as they
bounced into the air out of his way before settling once again
into the fragile dust and a new arrangement of shapes.

***

Pushing on towards the woods as his moment with the
hens faded, Martin had an unfamiliar sense of confidence and
control. He could hear running water before sudden shards
of memory sliced sharp and brutal through his senses. They
wiped out images of feathers and dust and warm sunlight and
instead he felt his mother's touch and heard his own whimpers
drowned in the sound of running water. Close by a cow was
drinking from a water trough with an automated filler on it.
In the hissing gurgling sounds a long-dead voice whispered,
'Let me help you.' Martin felt again her touch steal wet and
cold across the picture. An arctic cold bathroom, glittered with
white tiles, the cold tap running, chilled menace. The voice.
The sound of the water. Martin stopped dead in his tracks.
He heard the surging sound now easing, as the cow finished
drinking and stepped away. Martin was on his knees. The box
file had fallen to the ground and both hands were on his head
and pulling through his hair, and he was sweating, coughing
and shaking. 'It's done. It's done. Over. Gone,' he muttered.
And again, 'It's done, we're done, I'm done.' Then 'no more'
through locked teeth and, shutting his eyes and counting the

hens, the furrows, the fence posts and clenching his stomach, he stood as tall as he could. He bent to pick up the file and left his coat by the trough, seeing muddy water seep slowly into its perfect blue as he waded through the murky brown of a small stream that marked the edge of the woods, box file held high. He was in the woods near Shadowhurst, his woods, his space, but he saw no path, no direction, only forwards into the shadows, no steps to retrace, no returns.

Eyes half closed, Martin was aware of untold stories, shapes and colours. They surrounded him, still and fixed deep in the cool darkness. It was an unknown place of silence, textured and layered and full of distant whispers and congestion and yet still, the voiceless sounds of an impenetrable secret. To move forward at all he had to push hard through the brambles and jagged-edged ferns that reached out and clutched at him. It required some concentration for him to open his eyes fully to choose a way through the tangle. Wheezing a little, he negotiated a path through the mess of grasping undergrowth so resistant to disruption, so determined not to submit and so determinedly forcing his focus on every step, making it slow and deliberate and precise, falling not falling, stepping not stepping, binary once again.

His breathing heavy and his jeans stippled with thistle spikes, burrs and thorns, Martin's earlier tears had dried dusty and grey at the sides of his flushed face. He tried hard to think ahead, focus on forwards, the destination. As he tripped slowly through the tangled stems, his mind instead flipped through a muddled sequence of images of hens and cows, his coat slowly soaking up water, the puzzle of this wood's unknown shape. He tried to concentrate but his memory was squeezing at the pictures, pushing them out of the way to jump back and beyond to the places where the noises in his head would surely drown him.

He stood a moment breathing deep and wheezy in the torpid shadows and waited, counting his breaths, counting backwards to the furrows, fence posts and hens, counting the splashes of water from the trough as they hit the ground and he let himself be led to a place of darkness and fear. Trembling he saw the vision of her, the vision of the cold walls, the rising terror as she stared hard into his eyes, rubbing all the while the towel, rubbing so hard and whispering, touching him, pinching and crude. He stepped back and froze the image in his head and slowly saw himself moving around it, a statue in some grotesque gallery. And as he softly turned the image this way and that, he saw again her hands, red and spare, heard the emptying bath water gurgling down and away, felt the blackness of the night beyond the steamy windows, and saw the greyness in her dead face, the spaces in between the hairs on her head and the coffin waiting to be burned. He saw the rising fire licking and hissing to turn her from ice-cold grey into a hysterical riot of golden flames calming soon to amber embers and then smouldering just to dust. He remembered the silence after the preaching and the prayers, he remembered the muttering words of sympathy uttered by a stranger, he remembered that he was beyond her touch and remembered he would let his feet fall and know that they would land on solid ground. He stood still and heard the whisper of leaves, felt the brambles loosen and the ground hold him upright and steady, breathing, breathing.

Above the heavy wheeze of his battered lungs Martin was aware that ahead he could hear someone talking loudly, a monologue with no other voices. Occasionally, there was laughter and sudden bellowing shouts. As he walked slowly forward he was passing through less dense undergrowth and under a lighter canopy, and could see that he was coming in at an angle to the footpath. On his bottom sat a man dressed in smart tweeds, slightly dishevelled and decorated much as Martin was with mud splashes, dust, twigs, leaf and bramble fragments. His binoculars, festooned with members' enclosures tags from multiple racecourses, hung from a strap around his neck and stood to attention on the curve of a round belly. The belly was upholstered with large checks, the waistcoat partly unbuttoned and stained with what might once have been red wine, or some anonymous gravy. The bowler hat that lay upside down on the ground beside him was slightly tattered at the rim, its grosgrain band faded and worn, the pale green satin lining creased and variously patterned with a miscellany of sweaty traces. A long history. He was drinking from a battered silver flask and eating crisps from a bag torn open on the ground, within easy reach of his slender long-fingered right hand. He was smiling. His handsome face was pink and shining and lined with pleasures long since enjoyed. They were deeply etched around his eyes and mouth, from which a slow dribble of spit was ebbing.

As Martin scrambled out onto the path with his precious cargo, the man raised his flask in a polite salute. 'Welcome, m' friend, welcome to the shellibrayshn.' Martin, hot and puffing and still in a state of mild distress, stared silently at this jovial greeting. The man continued humming his little song, suffered a momentary gurgle of indigestion and continued to work on his crisps and the remnants of the flask. Martin matched what he saw before him as best he could with the similar scenes he had seen in London on his walks to and from the 93 bus stop and elsewhere. But this was not some homeless outcast with just enough money to get pissed. The probabilities were all wrong and no people were on hand to provide money, nor were there shops to spend it in. Martin, who was trying and failing to reconcile the incongruities of the scene, eventually said 'cheers' rather awkwardly back.

The man lolled comfortably against his tree, nestling into its bumpy curve, the outstretched buttress roots offering a cosy embrace that helped to prevent him falling over sideways. Through half-closed eyes and with immense dignity he said, 'I'mmos dreaflee sorry.' He coughed a small ahem in order to gather his thoughts and prepare the next few words, which he hoped would have spaces in between. 'But it's completely impossible... at this prissizetime.' Another small pause to regroup his syllables and to wipe carefully at the crisp crumbs peppering his cheeks, but adding more in the process. '...for me to welcome you proply because I abslootly cannot stand.' A long sigh masked an intense effort not to drift off into a doze. 'Up,' he said. At this point he raised his face to look squarely and decisively in what he estimated must be Martin's direction and with immense effort and concentration finished with, 'Aneven fi could, which is not even remoeleelikely, I would not bable to sto' myself fa falling back down again.' At this point the effort of conversation overcame him and the man passed out completely, letting his flask fall to the side, tumbling the upright binoculars almost into the crisps but for the strap around his neck. The coloured tags fluttered gaily and he snored a little snore. 'Rrrrrf', he said and 'rrrrrerf' in reply.

Martin stood still, watching this extraordinary performance and crouched down beside his fellow traveller to give his shoulder a gentle push. As suddenly as he had dozed off the man woke up and spluttered ''m fine, 'm fine', before scrabbling around frantically for his flask, sending crisp crumbs and edges swirling. 287, Martin noted as they fell, plus four for the neatly opened pack. Martin, still crouching, watched him as he took a pointless swig from the long-emptied flask.

'Don't I know you from somewhere?' Martin said, aware of a curious familiarity.

With a mock bow conducted with immense dignity from

the chin to the collarbone the man said, 'Julian Nettlesby esquire, at your service.'

'What, not John Nettlesby?'

'No. Juleeean. Brothnsober, 'cept for pint or two on Sattidy nights at Swan. Me' – with a thump at his chest – 'altogether diff kettle of...' And he dropped his head into his chest and once again fell asleep.

Standing there in the woods alone with a possibly dead old man sprinkled with crisp crumbs was a new experience for Martin and it took a moment for him to work out what should happen next. He looked at his phone and realised that he had no idea how to call an ambulance, but noted that it was getting late and cold under the rising wind. Darkness was beginning to squint through the trees and Martin's assessment was that this was probably not a good combination for Julian Nettlesby esquire. They were surrounded by woods, but they were on a path. A start. Running along the track, Martin could hear the sound of a machine droning tunelessly in the distance. As he burst out of the wood onto the open grass he could see Simon topping the edge of the field. That was what that bill for a new Kubota tractor was for, Martin thought, watching the machine's slow progress as it travelled ponderously along.

Watching Simon loop around and start heading towards him, Martin waved and shouted out. He heard nothing above the din of the machine, but Simon was surprised to see his boss popping out of the woods in front of him, without his velvet coat and waving maniacally. He saw he was carrying something. He considered turning off the motor, thought the better of it and carried on as if he hadn't seen the strange man beckoning from the woods. As Simon approached pretending to daydream, Martin lost patience and came at a chest-rattling run over to the mower.

'There's a man, a man passed out in the woods,' Martin

coughed. 'He says his name is Julian Nettlesby. He needs help. He might already be dead. He's ancient,' he panted as he spat copiously onto the newly topped grass.

Simon stared at the stain on his neatly trimmed sward and then at the woods beyond and calmly said, 'Don't you worry about him. He's probably had a win at the races. Was he all dressed up? Hat an' all? Binoculars?'

'Yes. How did you know?'

'It's what he does. Posh bloke version of his brother, he is, spends a fortune on the 'orses and usually wins like, he's got the knack see, studies the form, talks to the lads and work riders, and gets winners at long odds. That's why on race days we find him in the woods pissed as a fart and with pockets full of cash.'

Martin considered this for a moment. 'Do we just leave him there, then?'

Simon sighed. 'S'what we usually do but then it hasn't happened for a while and 'e is gettin' on now. I suppose we should get them up at the farm to collect him. Is he in the usual place, near that old sweet chestnut tree?' And soon he was on his phone calling Julian Nettlesby esquire's brother to send someone down to pick up the gentleman fallen asleep in the woods.

Sprawled on his sofa back at Shadowhurst mulling over the day's events and the excitement of his London triumph, Martin remembered the face and the encounter in the woods. The face was an echo of the face from the meeting in the pub with Joshua. The name Nettlesby was a similar echo, so he knew the name too. It was a surprise to come across a collapsed man in the woods, but Martin had been oddly unsurprised to hear his name. There was something more though, something that he couldn't place. This puzzle Martin turned over and over in his mind, listening to the Stranglers burbling about 'lies and deception, they move in one direction, and then in the end, in the end you lose' and sipping his Pol Roger. It was the first name that was resonating loudest in his mind, not the last. It was floating along, dancing on tiptoe and reaching out to tease at fragments of memory, shreds of ideas and vague images. And slowly it started to come into focus and he remembered why the name was already in his head, stored in another place but there. He had seen it printed and written amongst the papers in the steamer trunk. Julian Nettlesby was amongst the stuff in the box, stuff from another life and a lifetime, almost, away. He had seen him in a letter and in a diary and his name was in the box file of stuff he brought back from London, the stuff that Roger had found and given to him.

Looking through the list still on his desk didn't help. Looking through the stuff still on the floor was the only option, and Martin soon found the reference. It was in one of the diaries, for the 27th December 1944. 'The Nettlesby boys were here again sniffing round, showing off. Julian's too handsome for his own good and John's just plain sharp. Good riders though and gave me useful lead over the Dudswell ditch.' He found the draft of a letter to 'Darling Charles'. It had several lines crossed out, but mentioned seeing Julian walking in the woods, and that he gave her a bunch of primroses and that he was charming and helpful, offering a hand with the hospital, offering to drive people to and from the station. It was hard to tell under the scratchings out. This must have been a rough draft of a letter Ruth finished and later sent. But where to? There were other drafts, with dates all between the end of 1944 and March 1945. There were newspaper clippings too, stories about the Nettlesbys' work to support the war effort, stories about the elopement of Ruth Lorne and her family's distress.

But as before there was nothing much about Charles, just the photo and a few letters from him postmarked London and with various dates in the fading winter of 1944 to 1945, none of them later than March. In all of them he spoke of plans for the two of them and for how wonderful life would be for Ruth in Canada, of the children they would have, the adventures, the life once the war was over. In the diaries too there was much talk of Canada, of making a new start, of leaving a destructive and dead world behind and thriving somewhere shiny new and clean and away from decay and ancient history.

***

'Hey, Joshua, what's happening?' Glaring at the phone, Martin put it on speaker, as he continued browsing through the faded papers.

'Where are you?' Joshua shot back, his voice bouncing around the glass room like an angry wasp beating on a windowpane.

'Looking through the stuff from the trunk. I made it back from town on the train and walked from the station. Came across a drunk in the woods, and he's Nettlesby's brother. Slightly younger, I'd say.' Martin could hear his friend's mind chugging along, working its way through the many curious and alien new facts that had been presented. 'Are you still there?' Martin said, further confusing his friend.

'Yes, I'm bloody here, of course I'm here. I'm just gobsmacked that you made it home and that you took a train to get there. Why on earth did you do that? Why didn't you tell me you were in town? I was expecting to see you this week.'

The irritation in Joshua's slightly plaintive voice made Martin stop and wonder why, what's the problem? He coughed a cough of reassurance and said, 'Not sure, just needed to do it. I was in town to find out more about the house, and I did, that's all. You had most of it but Roger, you know, Alison's husband, he's found out a bit more. Not much and not very exciting, but it helps make some sense of the stuff in the box. Helps me get this place a little more. Come down tomorrow.'

At the other end of the phone Joshua was silent for another

unexpected moment, before spluttering, 'That's why I'm calling. We've some stuff to go through, quite a few things actually, including what you want to do about the garden there
and Alison's said you should have ponies. Probably wants them
for the girls. We should talk about it. I'll be down in the afternoon.' Joshua hung up and stroked his ginger beard, pen-
sive, watching the clock tick-tock, precise and slow, towards a
hopeful tomorrow.

***

The rain was coming down hard when Martin drove into
the station to collect Joshua. Seeing him laden down with a
heavy briefcase full of work, Martin was reminded that he
hadn't seen Joshua when he was up in town and that he'd
enjoyed the break. He hadn't done much except smoke, go to
bars and take the odd turn in the dark on Wimbledon Common. That might explain his belaboured breathing and was
probably why Joshua was so keen to come to Shadowhurst for
the weekend. There would be much to deal with.

Growling along the lane the car sliced its way through the
downpour back to the house. The views were looking less
closed and forbidding and the early summer flowers added
spots of colour to the darkness of the rhododendron crowds
running along the top of the stream bank.

'How do you like the view now?'

Joshua waited for his answer and eventually Martin said,
'What view?'

'We had the trees on the banks of the stream cleared and
widened so that you've got a better flow of water into the
lake. And you can see those rhododendrons when they flower,
which they are starting to do, see?'

'Rhodo-whats?' Pulling into the drive, Martin cut the engine
and strode up to the front door. Inside was warm and white
and still and when Joshua came in behind him Martin said 'take

off your shoes, please' before heading to the fridge and a Pol Roger. Joshua stared and stared, and then took off his shoes and placed them on a new shoe rack. Leather slip-on mules were waiting there and as Martin turned from the fridge, Pol Roger in hand, he said, 'Alison guessed they'd be the right size.' And they were.

The party

Some weeks after his encounter in the woods, Martin came back once more from his squalid flat and twilight life to Shadowhurst. Unwell and wheezy from too long in London, his aspect was that of the forgotten, the ignored and dissolute. Too many cigarettes, too many strangers, too many tuna fish sandwiches in Putney High Street, too much silence.

'Good to have you back, Martin,' Simon said as he shut the garage doors, watching his boss slope across the drive. 'Joshua's in there waiting for you; came by the lunchtime train. Said he hoped to catch you earlier.' This last with a hint of rebuke that Martin didn't notice. In answer he gave a violent cough and spat vigorously on the drive. 'Right,' Simon said as he turned and headed back to his mower.

In the kitchen Jodi was loading champagne and tins of tuna fish into the fridge. 'Almost done.' She smiled as she shut the fridge door and turned to Joshua: 'Well, I'm off, should've been gone long before his nibs got back.' Seeing Martin come through the door, she rolled her eyes and smiling wide said, 'Sorry about that, thought you were still outside with Simon.'

Martin looked on puzzled as she let the proffered cigarette end drop into her open palm. What did it have to do with her, he thought, noting the soft gleam of her smile and the brightness in the eyes. 'Don't forget Saturday. Barbecue. Here. Make sure you tell Sheila and Simon too.'

As Martin coughed, Jodi looked on wide-eyed at the outreach. Joshua stood up and held open the back door. He was smiling slightly at Martin's discomfort and stroking his beard in quiet consideration. He'd already told Jodi and Simon and Sheila that they might be needed on Saturday afternoon, and to keep it free. But he hadn't foreseen Martin extending any invitations.

Together on the terrace, they watched Jodi strike off across the lawn towards the lake and in the direction of Sheila and Simon's cottage, her hands deep in her pockets. Martin measured the long, confident stride and the swing of curly blonde hair dancing along with every unwavering step.

When the little red car had pulled into the drive, Jodi was getting ready to leave to join Sheila in the hops. Instead she waited, watching as Martin climbed out of the car, coughing and stubbing out his cigarette into the gravel. He had picked it up and handed it to her as he came into the kitchen coughing again. As she left without a glance back, she put the cigarette end absent-mindedly into her pocket and, smiling, headed for the hop garden, the reminder echoing in her head.

'That's exactly what he said. It wasn't a joke. He's definitely having a party.' Jodi's hands were grimed with hop oils, black and blending with the perpetual charcoal that stained her hands and nails.

'Well, I don't know,' Sheila mused. 'What's he, you know, thinking of, it's not what we do. I don't mind the extra hours, you know, like Joshua said, but we don't do that socialising thing.'

'I don't think he does either,' Jodi replied, laughing at the picture of this peculiar event in her head. 'He's thinking of you being there to work, I reckon, and me, but he's looking forward to it like. He's never had a party in his life I'll bet.'

Sheila pondered a while before observing, 'It'll be our party, won't it, look at it like that, it's our party and, you know, he's picking up the bill and paying us into the bargain.'

Turning to Joshua, Martin reached out a hand. 'Sorry I've been sort of absent. Again. No reason, not really.'

Joshua, smiling, took his curiously cold and limp paw. 'Good to see you. Missed you. But really it hasn't been so long. And I've been away with the squash team so no harm done.' The handshake was a novelty, the sorry getting less so. He held on just a little too long until Martin withdrew and cleared his throat, moving away.

Together they wandered through the house and its welcoming calm towards the courtyard. The afternoon sunshine's lazy rays were trapped in a riotous blaze of colours, dust and insects hovering before diving and swirling against the light's slow fade. Sheila and Simon had put a table and some chairs out here for their frequent coffee breaks, so Pol Roger in hand Martin took a seat and leaned back, soaking up the warmth, facing the light and wheezing.

'Amazing that you're still off the fags' was the best Joshua could come up with. 'Shall we get to the work or do you prefer to wait? It's not a lot, just some investment stuff to go through. And a couple of companies looking for financing. I think you've been suggested as a potential investor by the Blast guys. We should probably...'

Martin was watching birds bouncing into the warm air above the courtyard, diving at the flies and mosquitos and flying fast away in a single swift movement. 'Did you see that?' he said and Joshua replied, 'Swallows', and tried again.

Changing tack, he said, 'You remembered it's this weekend that they're coming?' Sipping at his 1982 Bordeaux he waited, eyes closed. Joshua was relieved that Martin had remembered, so all that planning wasn't going to turn out to have been a waste of time after all. Martin was oddly distracted. He appeared to be savouring the warming sun and the quiet and the delicate grapes of his Pol Roger bubbling and fizzing on his tongue. He eventually swallowed them down and broke into a deeply congested, rattling cough.

'Yes,' he wheezed, 'it's this weekend. You told me they'll arrive on Saturday morning for a barbecue and leave on Sunday. Jodi should be here to help out. And Sheila and Simon. I told Jodi and told her to tell them.'

Joshua smiled. Of course Martin hadn't previously informed all parties of the possibility of a barbecue at Shadowhurst. And of course, Joshua had. 'So we have time for the work. Good. There's only a bit to go through, but it's getting tight for deadlines. Is there anything I need to know about the flat? Is it in need of attention at all?'

'Actually,' said Martin, with some recollection and mild surprise, 'no, no there's not, I haven't been there much. It's probably fine.'

Joshua was working out what 'probably fine' meant and decided not to pursue it. He could see the trace of the last few weeks when the credit card bills came in. And he could see from Martin's grey complexion and damp, shaking hands that he hadn't been eating much, but had been smoking and drinking a lot. It would be hotel rooms, dinners that Martin wouldn't have eaten but some stranger would have. He sighed and stood up and, as the sun dipped away, went indoors to find a takeaway menu and the number of a cab he could call to collect and deliver the food.

Martin stayed still in the slow-growing gloom and finished the bottle before heading for his glass room to watch the rain as it started falling on the glass. The gleaming walls were turning slowly from gold to dusk to black, the colours caressing the space around him, and the rain a half-whispered tune. He went once more through Ruth's diaries and those half-finished letters with their impenetrable crossings out and alien references. Bright white inside the room and an exterior densely black, raindrops blended the spaces in between into something otherworldly.

Martin knew much more now, now that this endlessly wet summer was pushing on and the gardens dripped colours like forgotten memories, drifted dreams. But what he knew was not enough. He had the facts, dates, names, destinations. This was black and white, tangible, data evidenced, considered and understood. But there was something more, something that he could not grasp, something intangible in the story of his house and it held him fast.

***

Roger and Alison had come to call on Martin at the flat, not really expecting to find him. Alison had wanted to nose around. She wanted to do a damage assessment for the next time he went to Shadowhurst and the cleaning crew would be in. When Roger and Alison arrived, Martin was sitting at his desk drawing. More swans, and images drawn in black and white of the lake views from his glass room. Many lines of fencing seen like an upended stack of pancakes, a regiment spreading, marching across the space. Martin was repeating them over and over, the same images repeated over and over again, and challenging him to spot the difference in his own lines and spaces. It baffled Alison, but intrigued Roger, whose eye saw something more than the rhythmic pen strokes, strokes that Alison saw only as obsession.

They had brought with them a few more papers relating to Shadowhurst and more information about the history of the house. It was on the site of an ancient Elizabethan hall house, trashed in the 1600s, rebuilt in the early 1800s. Two hundred years of missing stories. They had paperwork about the estate's many holdings and interests in the nineteenth century, and about when it was first requisitioned in 1914, what it was used for and by whom. Their documents confirmed that it was also used to house refugees in the 1940s and as a school after the village school had been bombed out. They had further references to the owners' names and the names of the family members. Roger had come to understand in a queer way that what Martin needed was to know all of it, to know everything about the house. More specifically he understood that Martin needed to know about Ruth and Charles and about their lives. He thought he could see Martin looking beyond just the facts of these long-dead people and their demolished house, beyond the data.

It seemed to be catching and Roger was beginning to share the fascination. He too wanted to know how the story of Ruth and Charles ended. Some of what he had found was new, and there was something else, a minor yet evocative addition. It was an auction house catalogue of fitments and fittings relating to the sale after the war. It told the sad story of demolition and destruction, the end of an old life but with no beginnings for anything new. Listed was a 450-foot run of skirting board and a 50-foot run of dado rail. Numerous flights of stairs were catalogued, floor by floor and wing by wing. A cast-iron drip sink and a cast-iron interior stove brought with them images of fresh vegetables and cooking, afternoons spent nurturing the heat in draughty rooms against the frosty chill outside. And a mosaic floor 25 feet by 40 feet evoked pictures of an orangery filled with exotics and languid beauty, afternoon tea, cakes, madeira and hot cross buns. There were fifty thousand roofing tiles and another eighteen thousand weather tiles. The sale comprised 1,370 acres and two mixed farms with residences and cottages producing £917 per year but with an estimated value of £1,165 per annum.

Martin read through the list and noted the pleasure gardens, plus a sunken Italian grotto, a swimming pool with dressing rooms, and tennis courts, hard and grass. He held his breath, hearing the sound of his heart beating, but feeling only the sounds of a Shadowhurst from long ago. They echoed in the far distance and yet surrounded him. Looking up suddenly and wide-eyed at his sister, he had blurted, 'Come over on Saturday in a week and we'll do a barbecue. Simon said it should be dry and not windy for a change.'

Beyond her surprise Alison considered that Simon was learning irony too. She made a mental note to cross-check with Joshua.

Alison heard her husband say, 'Have you actually got a barbecue, Martin, I mean something to barbecue on?'

'No. Good point. Could you pick one up and bring it with you? Not sure it's my thing.'

Alison regained her composure and kicked into gear, finding refuge in the prospect of getting things done, a plan. 'Of course. We'll get something sorted out this week and I suggest you get Simon and Sheila to help.' She continued blustering, taking full hold of the line he had thrown. 'We'll bring the girls and stay overnight if that's all right with you?' A question punted more in hope than expectation was rewarded with a lazy 'yeah, whatever, it'll be fine'.

And Martin was already gone, looking through the list again, measuring out the forgotten Shadowhurst in his head, picturing the staircases and the wings, placing the roof tiles one by one in tidy rows in situ and then in neat piles on the grass, a lot number fluttering occasionally in the damp, cold air, flipping back and forth with a slight cracking sound and waiting for the hammer. 'Can you get Bill to come too? He hasn't seen the place. I'd like to show him my glass room. He can stay as well if he likes. Plenty of room. You can have the master bedroom.'

In the car they were briefly silent before both started speaking at once in an excited tangle of words. 'Is he getting better, do you think?' Alison asked as Roger eased the car out into the traffic and headed south.

'Well, he's not getting worse.'

'Did you see the state of the flat? It was basically fine. Messy and a bit stinky, but nothing near like it used to get. Except the cigarettes of course. We'll have to redo the carpet again.' Alison paused for breath before continuing. 'But don't get your hopes up. He's just as likely to change his mind about Saturday as to see it through. It's this new thing with the history of Shadowhurst. Once he's clear on it he'll probably go backwards again. Those swans were interesting though, weren't they?' She stared out of the window, watching the rain trembling down out of the grey to splash and splatter on the pavements. She nudged again. 'Those drawings he was doing, the swans, they were rather interesting I thought.'

Roger had a distant tone to his voice and a faraway gaze. His gaze saw the distant swans and something more than just black-and-white lines. 'Hmmmm,' he said.

***

'Will it ever stop?' Martin and Simon were standing in the garage. An enormous gas barbecue, recently arrived and swathed in polythene and cardboard, lurked behind them. It had a faintly martial air.

'Forecast is okay for this afternoon, so we'll be all right. Sheila's got old Nettlesby coming down later with the meat. We weren't sure what you'd want so 'e's bringing a few steaks and a couple a pheasant, some chickens, burgers and sausages for the kids. Joshua said there'd just be Alison's kids, didn't he, no more, that's right i'n't it?'

Martin stared out at the hushing rain. He was hearing its voices, marvelling at the sounds of it calling for quiet. He watched it chase away across the drive to pound at the house and beyond, bouncing its eager way across the lawns and down to the lake. Simon waited and Martin stayed silent. Away in the woods the small stream was churning, carrying water away from sodden hillsides and deep into the lake's waters. An aggressive and furious energy sent fast-moving ripples and bubbles hissing out across the lake's passive surface. The wind danced insistent, driving away the water bubbles to burst unseen into the surface. The bridge of grass separating each lake from its neighbour was already underwater, a few brave blades of grass stretched up to keep some brief contact with the light, while their neighbours had given up and were starting quietly to drown. Later when he was watching the little girls jumping from the bridge of grass into the lake, Martin felt strangely concerned. He had never before felt anxious about them, rather had ignored them, maintaining a permanent scowl on any occasion he was forced to share in their presence. He could hear them squealing as they hit the water, the shock as the cold grabbed at them and held them momentarily down in darkness before suddenly letting go, to release them back to the surface and the light.

Martin sighed and turning to the barbecue started pulling at its coverings and with Simon's help soon had it fully undressed. 'We'll keep it in here so if this bloody rain keeps up you can cook in the dry.' He squatted down to a companion box and fished out a range of large implements suitable he presumed for use in barbecuing. There was also a large crisply starched white linen apron with the word Napoleon for some reason stitched in the corner of its bib.

'Cook?' Simon said, looking at Martin in bafflement, his voice rising in tension. 'Cook? Me? I don' do cooking, sir, Martin, sorry, Martin, but don' do it at all, that's a step too far for me, Martin.'

And Martin, with a glimmer of amusement, saw sincere agitation in his usually unflappable gardener.

'Well, I'm not doing it, I wouldn't know where to start. You're good with machines, so you can get this thing going at least,' Martin replied matter-of-factly.

'That's different, sir, Martin, that's not the same. I can do that all right, but I b'ain't doing no cooking, if it's all the same to you.'

Martin pulled at his hair and squinting with his head on one side coughed short and sharp in response. He considered a moment and then said, 'No, of course not. No problem. We'll get Joshua to do it. He can wear this apron. Get Sheila to take it to his room. That and the tools and the control should suit him down to the ground. Alison can help. Good.'

Simon let his chin, chest and shoulders fall in visible relief, and together they went back to the comfort of staring at the rain. They saw somewhere on the far horizon a faint glimmer of silver seeming to wedge a minute space in the flat pewter sky. It hung slender and fragile amidst the tumult and hissing rain pounding the earth with drops like cannon balls. 'Right you are, I'll tell Sheila. She can let Alison and Joshua know. An' I'll see 'bout gettin' it going.'

Martin nodded, turned and walked back towards the house, head bowed, hands in pockets and hacking vigorously as he went. As he passed the house the rain was easing so he walked down to the lake to look at the swans. He'd done a full circuit before he found them and stood staring at the details of black-tipped beaks, the black nostrils and the black triangle linking the round black eyes to the yellow beak. Elegant contrasts to their white heads. Rainwater was dripping from their feathers but they stayed still, serene and unperturbed.

***

Joshua was dressing for the afternoon's excitement and fingering a large well-pressed apron that Sheila had placed on his bed. He held it up against his new blue jeans and new checked shirt. He'd seen them in a magazine, next to images of smiling people, and gleaming dogs and horses, with hamburgers piled up against a backdrop of brimming wine glasses and fields. Perfect. Once dressed, Joshua was on the phone confirming the arrival of two ponies, guaranteed quiet and safe for beginners to ride. Ideal for children. Bombproof. They had cost a small fortune in the way of such things: safe and quiet come at quite a premium it seems. But the tack, rugs and various other accoutrements had been included in the hefty price and they were due to be unloaded in the afternoon, ideally before Martin's nieces arrived. The sense of anticipation, of excitement at the prospect of a special surprise, was an unusual pleasure for a man more used to satisfying his own indulgences. John Nettlesby, who of course had found them for Joshua, would bring the ponies down in the horsebox along with the meat for the barbecue. Joshua found this image slightly disturbing and hoped there would be no mix-up. He put on the apron, gently touching the insignia, rising in pride for a moment and then went to see how the preparations were coming along.

He was pleased to see the kitchen a buzzing hive of activity, with much chopping and slicing underway. The radio was playing Elton John's 'Saturday Night's Alright' and Sheila and Jodi were singing along at the tops of their voices. They had put together coleslaw and potato salad and were discussing how to cook sweetcorn and if they needed additional vegetarian choices besides the bean and walnut salad.

'Chocolate cake should do all right for pudding,' they heard someone say. As he looked in quiet confusion at the unfolding scene, Martin's voice cut across the noise like a guillotine. They all jumped into silence. 'Roger will bring a cake. He's good at cakes, so we can have that.' Dripping in the doorway Martin shook his hair and brushed down his coat, puddling the cold slate and scowling. 'Nice pinny. When are the others arriving? I'm all wet.'

The blend of the obvious, the authority and the quizzical stopped Sheila and Jodi's chat and gave Joshua a momentary pause. 'Alison and Roger and the girls will be here by lunchtime and Bill I'm not sure,' he said, adding that 'the ponies will arrive in a little while and Nettlesby's bringing the meat at the same time, so don't mix them up.' Groans from Sheila and Jody echoed his chortle, but Martin just stared and carried on dripping on the floor.

His head was swimming and his brain felt too light to grasp another thought. He had the sense of some trace emotion creeping into his consciousness like a disease. 'Ponies? What bloody ponies? Joshua, what ponies?'

'You've forgotten, Martin, you said to get a couple, for the girls, so that they will have something to do down here. Don't you remember?'

Elton, still blaring about diesel trains, saw Martin out of the room and heading for a change of clothes and the quiet of his glass room.

A phone beepled somewhere in the noise of the kitchen and as Jodi turned down the Saturday night revels, they heard Joshua answer it. 'Bill should be here by early evening. He's coming from a business trip in Antwerp and he's bringing a crate of Belgian beer,' he said excitedly. But Martin was gone and Jodi and Sheila didn't much care who Bill was or if he came or not.

'Right,' said Jodi. 'Nice pinny,' and she handed him a glass of red wine. The picture was coming together.

Alison climbed out of the car carefully holding onto an enormous cake while Roger unbuckled the girls and got the overnight bags. 'Now don't forget, don't tease Uncle Martin and don't behave like hooligans.'

'It's Martin, just Martin' came the mocking chorus back. And as the little girls jumped out of the car they saw a horsebox turning away along the lane and then in the same view a pair of ponies scavenging in lazy arcs as they made their slow ways across the field. They stopped occasionally to lift their heads and look about them. The girls stood stock still in amazement, pink-cheeked, eyes wide and looking from their parents to the ponies back and forth in momentarily stunned silence.

'Ponies. Ponies, Mummy, there are ponies in the field, is this Martin's field, are they his ponies, can we ride them, are they for us?' And by this time they were jumping up at Alison, threatening her balance and her grip on the giant cake, while Roger headed off towards the house in search of their host.

'Would you stop bouncing about so, please, girls, it's heavy enough as it is, please calm down. Yes, it's Uncle Martin's field and, yes, those are his ponies and since there are a couple of saddles and bridles on the ground I expect you can ride them. But you'll have to ask.'

The girls raced off after their father to find Martin, just Martin. Alison struggled to open the back of the car to let the dogs out, forgetting the ponies until it was too late. Nettlesby's fencing kept them barking at the sheep netting while the ponies looked up for a moment and continued chewing. Fat chocolate Labs were no concern of theirs. Relieved, Alison took her cargo into the kitchen and handed it over to Sheila's care.

'Aye, aye, what's this, then. Weighs enough to feed an army, you know.' Smiling broadly Sheila put the triple-decker vanilla, chocolate and orange sponge with brandy cream and jam fillings in pride of place on the kitchen table. Jodi, elbows deep in the washing-up, quickly dried her hands and found a new cake stand. 'I knew this would come in handy. Jodi,' she said, reaching out to Alison. 'We haven't met.'

'Alison. Martin's sister,' she said back, taking in the fair curls and the stained cuticles, the unassuming beauty and that wide embrace of a smile.

'Jodi's been helping out while I've bin down the hops.' Sheila's explanation brought with it information and facts for Alison to catalogue, but also a curious sense of disappointment. She had no time to consider it because Roger was calling her to look at the giant grill he'd ordered for direct delivery. Sheila carried on plating up various cuts of meat ready to cook and Jodi put the finishing touches to the almost immaculate kitchen before pouring herself a glass of champagne and fishing a rollie from her jacket pocket.

***

Changed and sitting at his desk, Martin was rereading the 1945 diary, its last entry 'tomorrow' just a single word underlined three times and with a rash of exclamation marks. And 'Milk train – 03:58' in brackets. Milk? Before he sat down, he had watched the ponies being unloaded from an old-fashioned wooden horsebox, stepping carefully down the ramp and bouncing onto the drive before looking about inquisitively. John Nettlesby handed over the lead reins to Jodi while he removed their little travelling rugs, tail bandages and boots. They were soon in the field, heads down, sniffing the ground and trotting up and down along the fence. Their interest in their new surroundings was short-lived and within a few minutes they were grazing quietly, settled and at ease, meandering across the field. Soon Martin's nieces would arrive and he tried and failed to picture the scene.

Martin's head was buzzing. He went back to the noisy kitchen and, collecting a bottle of champagne, muttered that he was going for a walk. Sitting chatting with Sheila and Jodi, Joshua was still in his apron and holding forth on Belgian beer and Bill's significance.

'Right,' he said. 'Do you want comp—' but before he could complete his sentence the kitchen door was banged shut and Martin could be seen striding towards the woods, passing through the receding drizzle on a mission. They understood that he would probably not be back for the barbecue.

Aware that his sister and brother-in-law were arriving very soon Martin had turned his back on the scene. His head an angry hiss, he strode sullen and silent to the folly and sat down on damp and broken masonry. He was surrounded by rain-battered flowers, their heads bent and dripping, and gently bobbing as the raindrops drove them down and down. Battalions of stinging nettles stood swaying gently behind him, their heavy summer seed heads slightly bowed on stalks as thick as a man's little finger. As they moved in the occasional breeze they caressed Martin's back and though they barely touched him, they held him safe.

Martin took a slug of Pol Roger, wiping his mouth with his sleeve. He could hear the water running down across the polished white stones and watched it rippling urgently away towards the stream and then to the lake. Martin was not at ease. He sat on his stone, watching the story of his barbecue unfold, reluctant to see the people arrive, and yet keen to see them. He stared and watched as the shafts of sunlight split the grey into smaller fragments, working their way into the air, shining golden on the steaming surfaces. From his vantage point Martin could see the prospect start to smoulder as if on fire from within, a spirit shining and reaching out from the depths to welcome the light.

The girls' shouts and squeals pealed up to him in his green and flowered cave. Their parents were talking to Joshua, and Alison was struggling with the massive cake too small for its cake stand and surely chocolate as anticipated. Of course. Cake. Martin remembered Roger's hobby and made a silent promise to have a slice this time. Too often Alison had had someone clear away mouldering cake remains from his flat. The remains would be crawling with gleaming blue flies. They would be maggot-infested and decaying. The remains were usually still roughly cake-shaped, but tunnelled through by enquiring insects looking for nourishment and a place to raise their young. But that was in the flat, Martin reminded himself. Here it was different. He'd invited people to share his space, he was feeding them and he'd even considered his nieces' entertainment. He could see the barbecue, the tables and chairs, maybe the food, the drinks, all being brought out in the hope that the rain would stay stopped for a while.

The hugeness of it all was overwhelming and he felt lost in a flood of experiences and outreach. Alien sensations threatened to stretch from within and grasp his throat and squeeze and squeeze and squeeze until the rattling in his chest and the buzzing in his head were silent. Sitting in the damp, a cold near numbness pervading his buttocks, Martin breathed long and deep, the cackling splitting his breath into splintered hard shards, sharp and painful. Eyes closed he wondered what a milk train was and why it was the last entry in Ruth's diary. He pictured the page and counted the lines on the day and the lines for the month, the year, but what had happened next simply wouldn't come into focus. His concentration was shattered with the piercing sound of the little girls winging its way up to where he sat, somewhere between today and the 25th or 26th March 1945.

***

The shrieks brought with them reminders that whether it was cake or ponies, potato salad or barbecued steak, people or Belgian beer, today was new for him. The thought drove a beat in his brain and he pushed away the thoughts of milk trains and diaries. He started counting again, but this time the number of paces between him and the house, how many steps the ponies had taken from the gate to where they were now, noses in the lake, the swishes of their tails, how many crumbs there are in a chocolate cake, the brightness of the growing sunlight and how quickly it would dry the roofs and grounds.

He lost track of his numbers as he watched Joshua and Simon wheel the great cooking machine from the garage to the terrace behind the house. He could observe the emerging scene as Sheila and Jodi went back and forth to the kitchen. Then he heard the music. Someone had started the CD stack and he could hear the strains of a Chopin nocturne seeping slow and soft across the warming air. Martin closed his eyes and took as deep a breath as he dared. Static rising and falling, rising and falling.

***

'Get that thing going, would you?' Roger looked across in surprise at Joshua, uncharacteristically imperious in his pinny and waving his wine glass at the barbecue. It was a muddle of knobs and dials and complicated racks, and Roger stared at it and wondered where Simon was. Simon had given up trying to work out how to start the thing and had surrendered the field. It was just too complicated with its two ovens and a rotisserie, a domed lid and wheels. The barbecue had drawers and cupboards and multiple burners and was more mobile kitchen than barbecue. With no Simon in sight and Joshua urging him on with a wave of his Merlot, Roger shuffled reluctantly towards the barbecue to take up arms.

Unseen Simon had sidled up to Roger's elbow and was wondering aloud, 'How do you start the thing?' After a pause he added, 'And what does it burn?'

Sheila, busy with laying the table, pointed helpfully at the gas canisters. 'What about those. Where's Martin? He'll know.'

Joshua, his pristine pinny now slightly wine stained, raised his glass in the general direction of the folly and then burst into breathless chortles as Martin appeared, as if on cue, feeling slightly damp and strangely quiet.

'Here's the instructions. You can work it out,' he said, picking up a booklet resting helpfully on the lid of the barbecue and heading for the new outside fridge and another Pol Roger. When Martin came back, Jodi was reading aloud and Roger and Simon were jostling to get on with doing the doing. Two ageing men, channelling their inner hunters and gatherers, they were itching to make fire and sparking cinders. Joshua was now nowhere to be seen. Thanks to the gas tanks the grill was hot within moments and they were choosing what to put on it. Champagne in hand Martin stood watching them, a group of people who were strangers becoming familiar to one other, becoming friends perhaps. Was this how it happened? And he took a gulp and turned his gaze away. He fought hard to stay in place. He saw the food laid out on a long table, the plates, sauces, napkins, condiments and cutlery. Jodi saw him watching and wondered if he would stay or disappear again. Would he mind if she took charge of the girls and the ponies?

'Martin,' she called across the space, 'do the girls want to play with the ponies?' He had never been asked such a thing and looked up in some confusion as Alison chipped in. 'What a good idea.' And the little girls bounced around him squealing before suddenly stopping when they remembered that it was Martin, just Martin. They were nine and ten years old, tall for their ages, strong, with limbs like young saplings, too long and awkward, portents of willowy height soon to come. They stared up at him with fixed, excited eyes, the younger one chewing at a nail, and the older one trying to look cool, tossing her long hair from side to side, but bending and straightening her knees in a series of sharp jerks that lifted her heels off the ground. Martin was confused. What was it to do with him?

Alison coaxed, 'The girls would love that, but what do you think? If Jodi's willing, what do you think?'

Martin had only ever heard his sister tell him what he should think, so her coaxing did nothing to break his muddled silence until he heard Jodi through the fog of confusion call to the girls, 'Let's just do it, shall we.' And with a slight smile as she passed, she looked into the darkest blue and said, 'You'll be fine with that, won't you, Martin?' Off the hook he said, 'Yeah, fine, that's fine.'

The little girls chanted, 'It's Martin, just Martin', and hurried after Jodi.

***

By the time Bill arrived the party was in full swing, the ponies and their fearless riders sweating and filthy with the effort of getting the ponies to go faster, or indeed to move at all. The guests were tipsy and talking noisily about the intermittent rain, the food and the surprising sunshine, with the exception of Joshua, who was hammered and had nodded off in a lounge chair. The sun was dropping second by second and the sky had turned a hazy mauve, streaked with the beginnings of another thunderstorm. The air was thickening and becoming congested. Martin was once more in his room drawing ponies in thin curves, black on white, and capturing their bright grey dapples with stippled ink spots of varying sizes and identical in number for each pony.

Roger was the closest to the driveway to welcome Bill and warned him that Martin wasn't coping with so many visitors, but that was just as well because 'we're all enjoying ourselves far too much to worry about him'.

Bill took the offered glass of wine and as he followed Roger onto the terrace gave Joshua a little kick, toasting to Martin as he did so. 'The beer's in the car. It isn't locked.' It had been many months now since the desk arrived and Martin's daily routine had so dramatically changed.

Bill looked down at Joshua, who took a little while to focus before starting up in his chair and remembering who he was, or at least who he thought he was. He had never in his life had quite such a headache or felt quite so dizzy. 'Martin sindoors, 'llbe thrilled you've made it.' Together they passed through a wall of noise, Queen's 'Bohemian Rhapsody' shaking the house and barricading Martin safely in his clear glass space. 'Lookoo seear,' Joshua called, rubbing his eyes as they entered the room. He was beaming a purple-tinged smile, where wine had greyed his lovely teeth and settled in the corners of his mouth. He recovered his poise on the slippery floor just in time to prevent the dregs of red wine from sliding out of his glass and onto the soft amber beech.

Martin turned in his chair and stared, one hand on the desk and the other holding back his hair, his eyes wide and fixed. 'Bill. You came. Joshua said you were coming but I didn't think you would.' And to Bill's astonishment his one-time protégé got up and came towards him, open-armed and smiling. The open arms didn't go quite as far as a hug, but as Martin let them fall, the smile stayed in place. 'They've got food out there and you can meet the girls. You know the others, don't you? It's not really my thing, but I'll be out in a little while.' The manners were impeccable, and Bill was stunned.

Joshua slurred back, 'S'wot you said, s'wot you said ages ago and you're – hic, sorry – still in here. Still in here with your bloody swans... and now s'ponies too.' This last as he leaned over the desk, initially to get his balance but then caught by the unexpected beauty of the black-and-white curves.

'You're pissed?' Martin murmured with mild surprise. Standing back he took in the sight of the immaculate Joshua, stained pinny still loosely in place, swaying into the desk ever so slightly.

Joshua turned his head to look adoringly at Martin. 'I was waiting f'you to come back and waiting ganwaiting and I just thought I'd have the one, jus' the one, you know, in the kitchen with the girls and then, they gimme another, another, and I dinsee, then well, then, then, thas whas sappened. Thas it.' And he smiled broadly and cleared his throat as he tried his best to stand up straight. Instead, he wobbled slightly and wide-eyed, with some small sense of triumph, he leaned his full weight on the desk and raised his glass. 'To Martin, bringer of all light to swansan poniss.'

Martin's look of bemusement at this previously unseen Joshua was rapidly recloaked in his usual mask. Bill merely cleared his throat and looked about him in that peculiarly English way, looking at nothing, searching for something, anything, nothing to focus on. In the end some sense of camaraderie overtook him and he too leaned on Martin's desk. Joshua put his head lovingly on Bill's shoulder and continued smiling at Martin.

The three of them remained there suspended in a moment of unexpected weight, and one that none of them fully appreciated. Instead of turning away Martin put his hands on their shoulders, one each, and nodded. Joshua nodded back and gave a little snorting laugh. Bill put his hand on Martin's and smiled, though he wasn't quite sure what was happening. A barrier had fallen, but perhaps only for an instant. Bill gripped the desk, as much for reassurance as for an excuse to shift the curious moment.

'Ah, here it is,' he said, now giving it an encouraging little pat, as if the desk needed comforting in its new and alien surroundings. He stood up, hoping that Joshua wouldn't topple over. Joshua rebalanced and started fiddling with his bangles. 'Where it all began,' Bill added with an indulgent smile. He looked over at Martin, who was still staring at Joshua's beaming face, noticing the stains in the corners of his mouth and the silly smile as Joshua concentrated hard on keeping still.

'Joshua, are you all right?' Martin said, remembering those long-ago conversations about being friendly and caring; but he hadn't had to remember, the question had just come. 'Bill, is he okay?'

And Bill put his arm around Joshua's shoulders. Glancing at the drawings on the desk he noted a half-finished one with a dense black triangle sitting at the heart of a slender curve. To the triangle was attached a similarly dense black circle. 'He's just fine, just fine, aren't you, mate. You know, Martin, you're looking very well, very well indeed.' And he led Joshua gently away and back to the party. As they left the room Bill called back over his shoulder, 'And I like those ponies and swans you're doing, very nice, very nice. In fact, exceptional.'

***

Shadowhurst has six bedrooms, plenty to accommodate Martin's houseful of guests. After a long day kicking at ponies to get them going beyond a trot, trying to race each other and inevitably falling off on the downward slopes, the little girls were ready for their bath. Tired and only slightly bruised they disappeared with their parents, whose joint task it was to do bath time. For Roger it was a means of ensuring that he worked only so hard and spent time with his girls, and for Alison it was a necessary ritual, something they had to share, had to do together, though she never really understood why this mattered so much to her. Bill and Joshua found their way to their bedrooms, Joshua by now fully sober and slightly embarrassed and still wearing the pinny, albeit sideways, Bill well fed, slightly drunk and still processing his business meetings of the day before. He lay awake until the Belgian beer took over and he succumbed to Leffe- and Chimay-tinted dreams. Simon, Sheila and Jodi walked across the soggy fields, stopping to pat the exhausted ponies and to work out where the still submerged land bridge was. The wind was picking up again.

When all was quiet Martin sat on the terrace with one more glass of wine and another tin of tuna fish, another slice of chocolate cake. He watched the glowering heavens and the rolling clouds, the distant lightning flashes and the far-off snarl of thunder. The air swirled around him, frightening off the insects and even the bats. The sky was coming down lower and lower, the clouds wreathed in dark greys, purples and blacks shot through with sudden silver. The thunder bellowed ever closer and soon the sky could hold on no more and the clouds, torn and ripped with sudden ferocious lightning claws, let go. The water fell heavy and dense, like stones smacking hard and hostile on the terrace and everything else. The world was submerged in a nether space of air and water churning all around and obliterating all the lines between, and there was only turbulence and grey.

The wind worked hand in hand with the clouds and water, thrashing every surface, tumbling furniture, tearing down the flowers and small trees, wrenching at branches, turning shrubs in upon themselves and hurling vicious punches at everything in its path. Swirling dervishes hauled at the lake's surface, and Martin was sure he could hear the sound of trees falling in the woods, of rocks and stones tumbling, of earth shifting and sliding away to make a different landscape. He stood up, drenched and shivering, and thought he saw in the distant shadows a change in the contour of the treeline. Dancing under the lightning flashes, he saw a wild silhouette leap like a marionette, its distant strings pulled and snarled to suddenly let go and see the marionette fall, a marionette no more, just a tangle of wood and fibres. The sound was symphonic. The howling and screaming wind, the groaning of the trees and the hush of the falling rain called for calm. But there would be no calm.

Back in the house the little girls were muddled together under the covers in their parents' bed. Roger and Alison had drawn back the curtains to watch the display, keeping their children safe between their own warm bodies. Joshua was mildly annoyed at the noise and planning his outfit for tomorrow and wondering when he and Martin would get to the work. It needed doing, and it would be good to get back to town on Monday, in time for his squash game. Bill was deep asleep and didn't notice the storm. He was dreaming about the job in Antwerp, about how he would prepare the drawings for the renovated central station, if it would happen. In his dream he was living in Antwerp, eating Belgian food and drinking Belgian beer and much chocolate. He was trading diamonds, getting lost in twisted streets, riding a bicycle everywhere, and all forever more. Martin swizzled his way somehow into the dream and offered to add swans and ponies to the walls of Antwerp's central station.

***

Martin didn't go to bed that night but stayed on a retrieved sun lounger with a blanket from his sofa. He had positioned the sun lounger at the opened French windows, amidst the rain and wind, and he barely slept, listening instead to the wind screaming through the night. He heard his nieces squealing in the dark and then giggling. Somewhere in his half-sleep images he saw Ruth and her mother standing on the steps of Shadowhurst, umbrellas raised. He remembered the names of the hospital patients and their doctors and nurses. He remembered the Nettlesby brothers and how many metres of post and rail fencing and sheep netting he had paid for. He saw his flat, immaculate and newly carpeted, ashtrays strategically placed, and he saw Wimbledon Common sodden and dangerous in the rain, the Mere overflowing, the road traffic intermittent and the spaces unpeopled.

By dawn Martin had shut the French windows and made his way back into the house. He was deep asleep face down on the sofa and stayed there until the smell of coffee and warm almond croissants reached out to rouse him. He stood up slowly, yawning and wondering if the noise in the kitchen was something he could realistically face. What time was it? Were they all out there? He turned away from the shadowy light pushing its way through the windows and tried to go back to sleep.

Ruth

But it was no good, so wrapping himself in the damp blanket Martin went in search of hot coffee. The kitchen was mayhem, with toast burning on the Aga and Alison trying to persuade Roger to 'just sit down, would you. I've got it', wrestling with the toaster and an oven glove.

The little girls were chattering and excited. 'Martin, just Martin can we play with the ponies again? It's stopped raining and they've had a long rest and we have to go home later, so please, please?'

Joshua was manhandling a large coffee pot, positioning its lid and plunger with careful precision. 'Let your Uncle Martin, just Martin, wake up, girls. He's had a rough night of it by the looks of things.'

'Where's Bill?' Martin mumbled, reaching for a warm croissant and scraping a chair within reach of the table.

'Gone. He had to get back to town. Asked if you wouldn't mind letting him have a couple of your swan things. I told him I'd check and let him know.'

'What would he do with those?' Inhaling particles of warmed icing sugar, Martin exploded into a fit of coughing and tears, much to the delight of his nieces.

He took his croissant and coffee and stepped out into the garden, where strong morning sunshine was turning the wet terrace into a mess of primordial haze. Steam was rising, and as he looked across the lawns and down to the lakes he saw that the small strip of land that had joined the lakes together appeared to be no more. It was too far away to tell, but he could see the savage gash of the banks on the nearside lake where the water, long dammed and checked, had suddenly broken through, bringing the dividing strip of lawn along with it. Martin set off at a slow pace towards the lake to get a better look. He noted the graceful progress of the swans, moving carefully along the far edge, pausing here and there to poke at the reeds, dipping an occasional beak into the dense black waters. He muttered softly to himself, 'They were Shakespeare's favourites: "…and wheresoever we went, like Juno's swans, still we went coupled and inseparable". Was it *As You Like It?*' he wondered aloud, squelching his boots into the sodden grass, sending up tiny bubbles with each step.

***

The swans were moving slowly in the direction of the woods, pushing against a gentle current. The barrier between the two lakes had collapsed, Martin was certain, so he hurried along to where the join used to be. He was looking down at the water all the while, uncertain where precisely the edge of this side of the lake was or how deep the blurred brown line was as it crept slowly up towards the house. He reached the spot where just yesterday the little girls had been jumping into the water and saw that the bridge had indeed disappeared, the earth ripped through. The sun and warmth slid together behind a silver-edged cloud and Martin shivered as he looked up to the sky and to the horizon line of his woods. The trees were leaning black and flat against the light, newly rearranged. He remembered his impression in the night of a massive movement of trees and of the sodden hillside appearing to slowly move under the force of the storm. Now he could see that the weight of the waterlogged soil had been too much and that the slope, along with its forest of newly thinned rhododendrons and stacks of logs, had together slid inch by inch down the hill, water and sod pushing slowly towards the lake's edge to press its mighty weight down into the water. It was this force that had pushed aside the bridge, Martin concluded, turning back at the echoes he thought he heard. They were calling him, calling to ask about the ponies, which Martin had forgotten about.

'Yes. Yes, if you can find them,' he yelled.

'There, over there near the edge of the lake,' Roger called back. 'The girls can get them.'

Martin looked across to where they were pointing to see two silver shapes bright against the dark mud and the tangle of wet roots and twisted limbs. White on black he thought and watched as the two ponies nuzzled along the ground and picked their way through the puddles. He was reminded of a fairy tale from long ago, a fairy tale about a unicorn and a little boy who could ride away on the unicorn if he promised to keep secrets and never tell. As he looked, Martin was struck by the curious complex shapes of the tree roots, twisted sinews curling up out of the water and mud, stretching to reach the sky. They were draped with debris, tender branches snapped and hanging lifeless, destroyed and reformed into bizarre and ghastly decorations.

***

Martin watched the ponies for a while before marvelling at the mess the weather had made of his woods beyond; the black twisted roots and branches gradually coming into focus. They moved and shifted in the rising light, strange shadows and then sharp black against the light of the sky. And then he saw.

Turning towards Roger and the girls he bellowed with all

his force, 'Keep the girls up at the house. It's too dangerous.' Martin was yelling as loudly as he could manage, coughing and choking, vomiting slightly, as he staggered up the hill frantically waving his arms.

Roger, with a child on either side, was walking down towards Martin and the ponies. 'What's happened, old man? What's the matter?' he called, jolly and innocent.

Martin was halfway up the slope. 'Send the girls back,' he shouted through his choking cough. 'They need to wait in the house, and you need to come here now.'

The urgency was clear and alarming and although Roger couldn't see any problem, he thought it best to go with it. The ponies were clearly fine as they were already meandering up the hill towards the girls in hope of breakfast. 'Go back up to the house and get them some treats,' Roger said. Adding helpfully, 'They'll like that, there's good girls, and tell Mummy that you should all stay up there until I find out what's bothering Martin.'

'Martin, just Martin,' they parroted in unison before walking slowly back up the hill, the ponies following along nudging at their backs as they went.

Roger sighed and rubbed the back of his head as he slowly walked towards the lake's edge and the woods to see what all the fuss was about. Martin had his back to him and as Roger drew closer he could see what Martin was staring at. At the heart of a tangle of branches and roots, a mummified corpse was tenderly embraced. Martin and Roger stood side by side, the horror mesmerising and compulsive. Pale skin stretched and distorted under sodden clothes, hanging from the body. Small white fingers twisted into claws, hands and forearms held up in pathetic supplication, the body a foetal curve. Dark hair plastered the bleached white face, and the eyes and mouth were marked sharp in hard black lines. She rested still and safe in

the slender branches. Spidery and black they cradled their bur-
den, holding safe the hideous offering. The two men stared,
rigid with horror. She wore a skirt, a blouse and a short jacket;
one shoe was still in place. The other shoe, its laces still intact,
hung from the tip of a branch. Crows were perched on the
branches, trying to reach down to pluck and pick at the juicy
bog-preserved remains. They stretched in vain to reach the
rotted scraps of clothing and as the sun forced through the boiling greys of rainy skies, the stark blanched face gleamed in the
sunlight. Telling a tale long since forgotten, a gruesome lip-
less gash of a mouth, teeth bared, was whispering. And around
the neck they could see a chain with a small gold heart washed
clean by the rain.

'Ruth.' Martin's voice was a husky wheeze as he and Roger,
rigid and immobile, stood caught in a horrible spell. They
watched a crow push through the snagging branches to pluck
at a shred of skirt. Martin clapped his hands and the crows rose
up, cawing and complaining, black shadows against the sky's
churn.

'What did you say?' came Roger's breathless whisper. Perplexed and confused he was trying to put together the pieces,
match the lines between one moment and the next, to understand how they could be sharing the same space with his happy
little girls and their ponies and such sudden, unbidden horror.
A dead woman preserved in airless sludge had been horribly
exposed, wrenched from her muddy tomb to gleam bright and
innocent in the Sunday morning sunshine.

'Ruth,' said Martin again. 'It's her, it's the girl who used to
live here, the one that ran away with the Canadian airman. It's
all in the papers, the papers you gave me, it's all in there. She
didn't run away at all. She probably never even made it to the
station. And the milk train in the diary, that's what it means, a

train. Milk train – 03:58. That's it!' This last with a shout that made poor Roger almost jump.

'I think we need to call the police,' he replied, subdued and sensible. 'Wait to do that until we're gone. I'll explain to Alison, but I don't want the girls to see this, to even be aware of it.'

'Right,' said Martin, still staring at the dead girl. 'We'll handle it. I'll let you know later what's happened. Go. No, wait. We both should go.' They turned away and started up the hill to the house, frequently looking back, drawn inexorably to stare and stare again.

Dazed and barely able to focus on what they had agreed, Roger put his arm around his wife and quietly said, 'We have to go. I'll explain. Get the girls into the car. Now.'

Alison twisted to look at her husband and saw tears were welling as he raised his eyes to look at the sky. 'What's going on?' she ventured and was surprised to feel a slight push in the small of her back as he turned away and stood shoulder to shoulder with Martin. Alison hurried to collect their things, round up the dogs and children, and find the car keys. Roger stood with Martin on the terrace still shoulder to shoulder in the rain, coloured the same ashen shade, tears in their eyes, looking into the middle distance almost in a trance.

The girls finished their second breakfast and clambered complaining into the car. 'But, Mummy, why can't we stay some more? Why?'

Alison reminded them that Martin likes to be quiet and that yesterday had been a very busy day. 'But you said, you said we could play with the ponies some more. You said.'

Alison nodded and added, 'I know, girls, I know, but the ponies are tired.' Then, 'It's half-term soon.' Alison, faux jolly and bright, under control, her brain turning over and over. She focused on the girls, on some other day. 'When school breaks up we can come back and maybe you can camp out in the field with them. You could bring your friends as well. Won't that be nice.' Alison's mind was in chaos, conflicting facts and promises. Martin might not want them camping. He might not be here. The ponies might be on loan or lame. The rain might still be falling. She must talk to Joshua. She should ask Sheila. She should check with Roger. She needed data, facts, information, she must find out, must know what had happened. And what would happen next. Her breathing wispy and shallow, she felt dizzy watching Roger make his way across the drive, looking over his shoulder with every other step, almost as if he were running away.

Joshua, in shorts and rugby shirt, was still in the kitchen finishing his long and languorous breakfast, oblivious. His head felt a trifle heavy but in every other respect Joshua was back to his usual immaculate self. He was pondering how much work they should do before sloping off up to the pub for lunch, when Alison and Roger said they were on their way. 'Loads to do before the weekend's over, old chap.' But Roger's pale face and glancing eyes didn't match his hearty farewell. Joshua assumed a rare row of some sorts. Alison was frowning, calling the dogs to the car and trying to say goodbye all at once, not looking at him nor at Roger. Row definitely, he thought.

'Good job you've got all this sheep netting,' Roger observed for no particular reason and with a forced chuckle.

Joshua looked back slightly confused and said, 'Er, yes, I expect so', still wondering what Roger was on about, and why. Martin had joined them and was nodding wide-eyed, a pale and fragile robot. To Joshua's mind that was normal, even though normal had been changing of late. He sipped at his coffee and watched Alison and Roger hurry out of the kitchen and into the rain and their car. Moments later they were gone, and Joshua was going back to his breakfast. But as he reached for his cup, Martin burst towards him with his fists clenched and his eyes boring into Joshua's face. Martin hissed, 'Put that down and get some wellies on. Now.'

The insistence was more than urgent and the usual imperative tone terse and aggressive. Joshua was a little anxious. For all Martin's intensity he had never been like this, this hostile, dangerous even. Joshua crammed the rest of his coffee-soaked almond croissant into his mouth in one go and jumped up.

'Right. I'm there. I'll just get my boots,' he mumbled. They were still in his room in their box, fresh from an expensive outlet in town where he had spent a happy afternoon shopping for clothes and accessories for this weekend. He pulled them on, glad for the opportunity to wear them. Pausing only briefly to make sure his beard was free of pastry crumbs, he hurried down the hill after Martin, who was already halfway to the lake. In a series of short, little skips, he skirted the ponies, who seemed to have him marked out as a source of snacks, until he turned and shouted at them to go away and leave him alone. The ponies interpreted this instruction as a definite no, as far as snacks and treats were concerned. They ambled off to continue grazing. Joshua, struggling in the unfamiliar footwear, found that side-stepping rather than skipping made it somehow easier to get down a wet slope at speed in wellies.

As he once more approached the rearranged woods, Martin was convincing himself that the ghastly apparition was just that, an apparition, even though Roger had been there with him. They had both seen it. But perhaps it was just a trick of the light and contorted branches, a false picture falling out of the chaotic image of a dramatically different landscape. A deception made of light and dark. Perhaps it was just rags not a clothed girl wearing only one shoe. Surely it wasn't real, it just wasn't real. It couldn't be. But standing again at the lake's edge Martin saw that it was. It was very, very real. When Joshua had almost reached Martin's side he slowed his pace and stared up in horror. One hand and then the other slowly rose to his mouth. As Joshua's gold bangles fell back against his wrist a delicate tinkle pierced pinprick notes in the silence holding them. They stood side by side and Joshua, feeling the tears welling up, could say nothing.

'The police,' Martin whispered. 'Get the police. I don't know what else to do. Isn't that what we should do? I don't know.'

Joshua nodded slowly. 'Yes, the police. And an ambulance. We need an ambulance too.' Joshua's hands shook as he tried to tap with slippery fingers. 'What do I say? Martin, what do I say?'

Martin turned away and could not answer. Joshua followed and recovering some of his composure he answered the questions put to him.

'We've found a body,' Martin heard him say. 'A woman. Dead in a tree. Yes. I'm sorry but that is what I said. Dead in a tree. No, she's not breathing. No, she's not conscious. She's dead. Dead, do you hear?'

***

The rest of that day was a blur, filled with police enquiries and gawpers from the village, including Simon, Sheila, Jodi and John Nettlesby, who pondered philosophically, 'so that's where she got to'. Sheila and Simon were holding one another's hands tightly, Sheila with her other fist at her mouth and Simon's face a blank. Jodi, horrified at her own distance, was making a mental image of the sight, readying herself to get it down later in black and white, wondering if she could capture fully its awfulness and its drama. Martin and Joshua were in control and focused, talking to the police, learning that there would be an inquest, and everyone was wondering how the body came to be there. They all agreed that it was Ruth and all of them had wildly different pictures in their heads of how she ended up mummified in mud for over fifty years.

The air at the lake's edge was a mass of competing dialogues, fragments, words, emotions hanging almost tangible in the sunshine, all laid bare like the washed white face suspended there in the tangled branches. It was clear that she had been preserved deep in a knot of rhododendron roots and dense anoxic mud. It was clear that over the years these root structures had broken and twisted around the corpse, holding her tight in their arms, preserving her in the ooze. The ferocious storm had dragged the nurturing trees and swampy hillside reluctantly down to the water and with them an awful secret was pushed unexpectedly out into the light and washed in the night's summer downpour.

The day's brief respite from the rain had been short-lived so the police teams worked fast, racing the weather to complete their reclamation. It didn't take long for the forensics team to make their preliminary assessment and for the body to be extricated and reclothed in a new black plastic shroud, golden heart and all. In fascination, people had followed every step as the body was moved up the hill into the ambulance. The people had faded away, but Martin and Joshua stayed at the lake, mindless, still in shock. They were standing where the lake had overflowed into its neighbour, when Joshua noticed something moving near the reeds. It was a small rectangular shape, a suitcase, and it was floating closer and closer to the swans.

'Martin, look,' Joshua half whispered, hurrying along the lake's edge as the wind started to pick up and the rain to fall again. Despite the wellies Joshua got to the suitcase first and together they hauled it out of the water, setting it upright on one of its short sides to let the water flow out. The initials were barely visible under the mud's black stains but there they were: RML. Ruth Margaret Lorne.

'Shall we hand this over?'

'No,' said Martin quickly. 'Not yet. Let's get it dried out at least.' He walked swiftly back to the house to shake the hands of the officers and to find out what happened next.

'We'll be in touch, sir. And we'll look into what you said about the identity.' But Martin wasn't sure if they meant it.

***

The letter arrived a few months later, telling Martin that the remains were now considered to be those of Ruth Lorne, but that no next of kin had been found. Efforts to trace the Canadian airman had produced no results. There was no record of a Captain Charles Hickson in the UK or Canada. Forensics found no injuries and death by drowning was presumed. The police confirmed there were no signs of foul play. The letter invited Martin to visit Inspector Roland Tatlock for further information and, if he wanted, to claim the remains since they were found on his property. Martin put down the letter and looked out at the lake and watched a shimmer of breeze skip across the water. He saw the swans moving into the shimmer and heard the tap of branches against his glass ceiling. He texted Joshua to tell him to plan a visit to Sussex police in Lewes as soon as possible. He texted Roger to tell him it was indeed Ruth. He called out to Jodi, 'Come and have a look at this.' And he felt the tears slow and hot welling from his eyes to run sudden and unexpected on his cheeks. He looked over at the suitcase still unopened in the corner, and looked at the lake and wondered when the swans had returned from their tundra excursion and when they would leave again.

Looking out at the frosted grass, Martin saw the bitter blue of the gleaming sky. He saw the ponies breathing winter steam snug and warm under their rugs. He saw the naked black trees reaching into sapphire heavens, their sparse beauty fragile in the reflected mirroring light. They shifted and wavered as the sun worked its slow way, far beyond the horizon, and he remembered his drawing. He dropped the letter to the floor and picked up his pen, as Jodi put his coffee on the desk and retrieved the dropped letter.

Martin's lines were slowly shaping as his hand moved with careful deliberation. As she turned and left the room Jodi said over her shoulder, 'You should show some of that, it's really not bad.' Martin turned with a scowl before realising that she was teasing him. And then, scrabbling through the mess of drawings strewn across the floor, he found one of the swans. He put it up against the coffee cup and stared at it a while, seeing in its lines the images of the days when they were drawn, a kaleidoscope of memories, their colours vibrant and loud, music playing, a riot of pictures dancing in his head. The pictures were pictures not data, imaginings not just ideas. He took the picture and held it at arm's length, his head on one side. Slowly smiling he placed it face down on his desk and with a thick-nibbed Rotring wrote 'To Bill'. He paused a while, wondering what he should put next. Halfway through another text to Joshua confirming the police station visit, Martin picked up the pen again and added 'with thanks and affection'. He finished the text to Joshua and sent it. Then he came back to his note. He paused, staring at the black and white, his eyes following the contours of the letters, marvelling at their sharp edges, the contrasts of shape and shade. Martin put down his pen. Then hesitantly he picked it up again before adding with a shaky hand '…and for helping me find an end and a beginning. With love, Martin.'

Acknowledgements

Thank you to all the people who have supported this book and its extended journey. Thank you to Xander Cansell for saying, 'Do you have some more of the manuscript you could send over to me to read through?' Thank you to Helen Francis for the insightful structural edit and to Jill Sawyer for the careful copyediting. Thank you too to Julia and Anna at Unbound for their professionalism and extreme patience. And thank you Paul for reading, rereading and rereading again and again and again.

Unbound is the world's first crowdfunding publisher, established in 2011.

We believe that wonderful things can happen when you clear a path for people who share a passion. That's why we've built a platform that brings together readers and authors to crowdfund books they believe in – and give fresh ideas that don't fit the traditional mould the chance they deserve.

This book is in your hands because readers made it possible. Everyone who pledged their support is listed at the front of the book and below. Join them by visiting unbound.com and supporting a book today.